KATE MULVANY is an award-winning playwright and screenwriter. Her new play, *The Rasputin Affair*, was shortlisted for the Griffin New Play Award and the Patrick White Award and will premiere at Ensemble Theatre in 2017. In 2015, she penned *Masquerade*, a reimagining of the much-loved children's book by Kit Williams, which was performed at the 2015 Sydney Festival, the State Theatre Company of South Australia and the Melbourne Festival. Her autobiographical play, *The Seed*, commissioned by Belvoir, won the Sydney Theatre Award for Best Independent Production in 2007 and is currently being developed into a feature film. Kate's *Medea*, created with Anne-Louise Sarks and produced by Belvoir in 2012, won a number of awards including an AWGIE and five Sydney Theatre Awards. It completed hugely successful seasons at London's Gate Theatre and Auckland's Silo Theatre. She's also currently under commission at Sydney Theatre Company. Kate's other plays and musicals include *The Danger Age* (Deckchair Theatre/La Boite); *Blood and Bone* (The Stables/Naked Theatre Company); *The Web* (Hothouse/Black Swan State Theatre Company); *Somewhere* (co-written with Tim Minchin for the Joan Sutherland PAC); and *Storytime* (Old Fitzroy Theatre), which won Kate the 2004 Philip Parsons Award. Kate is also an award-winning stage and screen actor, whose credits include *The Seed*, *Buried Child* (Belvoir); *Blasted* (B Sharp/ Sheedy Productions); *Tartuffe*, *Macbeth*, *Julius Caesar* (Bell Shakespeare); *The Crucible*, *Proof*, *A Man With Five Children*, *King Lear*, *Rabbit* (Sydney Theatre Company); *The Beast* (Melbourne Theatre Company); *The Literati*, *Mr Bailey's Minder* (Griffin Theatre Company); and the feature films *The Little Death* and *The Great Gatsby*.

CRAIG SILVEY grew up on an orchard in Dwellingup, Western Australia. He now lives in Fremantle, Western Australia, where, at the age of nineteen, he wrote his first novel, *Rhubarb*, published by Fremantle Press in 2004. In 2007, Craig released *The World According to Warren*, a picture book affectionately starring the guide dog from *Rhubarb*. In early 2008, he completed his second novel, the award-winning *Jasper Jones*, which has become a hit around the globe—it has been published in over thirty countries and has been translated into fourteen languages. *Jasper Jones* has won Australian Book Industry awards, Australian Independent Booksellers awards, the Australian Booksellers Choice Award and was a co-winner of the West Australian Premier's Award for Fiction. The novel also won the 2012 USA Printz Honor Book for excellence in literature written for young adults. *Jasper Jones* has been shortlisted for the Miles Franklin Literary Award, IMPAC Dublin Literary Award, and both the Victorian and NSW Premiers' Literary Awards, among others. In 2016, Craig co-wrote the AWGIE-winning adaptation of the *Jasper Jones* feature film. Craig followed up *Jasper Jones* with the acclaimed and beautifully illustrated novella, *The Amber Amulet*. Outside of literature, Craig is the singer-songwriter for the band The Nancy Sikes.

Guy Simon (left) as Jasper and Nicholas Denton as Charlie in Melbourne Theatre Company's 2016 production. (Photo: Jeff Busby)

BASED ON *THE* NOVEL
BY CRAIG SILVEY

ADAPTED FOR THE STAGE
BY KATE MULVANY

Currency Press, Sydney

CURRENCY PLAYS

First published in 2016
by Currency Press Pty Ltd,
PO Box 2287, Strawberry Hills, NSW, 2012, Australia
enquiries@currency.com.au
www.currency.com.au

This revised edition first published in 2017

Cataloguing-in-publication data for this title is available from the National
Library of Australia website: www.nla.gov.au

Typeset by Dean Nottle for Currency Press.
Cover design by Alissa Dinallo for Currency Press.

Currency Press acknowledges the Traditional Owners of the Country on which
we live and work. We pay our respects to all Aboriginal and Torres Strait
Islander Elders, past and present.

Contents

Tom Conroy (left) as Charlie and Charles Wu as Jeffrey in Belvoir's 2016 production in Sydney. (Photo: Lisa Tomasetti)

INTRODUCTION

1965 will be a tumultuous year for the small town of Corrigan. The race to the moon is underway. Australia's involvement in the war in Vietnam is being escalated and some of the young men are being conscripted and sent over to fight in it. And fifteen-year-old Laura Wishart has mysteriously disappeared. For Corrigan the last event overshadows the others. What happened to her?

For Charlie Bucktin this summer will be traumatic and life-changing. This play, like Craig Silvey's much-loved 2009 novel on which it is based, starts like a good detective story with the discovery of a body but it soon becomes something else. In the thrilling opening scene Charlie is woken in the night by Jasper Jones, the slightly older and much tougher outcast boy, and taken to his secret place outside town where he has found Laura's body hanging from a tree. For reasons that are shocking but completely understandable they cut her down, weigh her body with stones and sink her in the dam.

It is from that initiating act that the play starts to depart from the detective genre. There are no detectives, only the police who, like the townsfolk, mindlessly blame Jasper for everything bad that happens in Corrigan, and when it comes to the crunch are happy to violently beat him up because he is a 'half-caste'. Only Charlie and Jasper know what has happened to Laura's body, and they keep their secret till the end, hoping to find out the how and the why of it all.

This is a play about trust and courage, especially among the five wonderful central teenage characters. Jasper believes he can trust Charlie, which is why he seeks his help in the first place. Charlie finds to his surprise that he almost instantly trusts Jasper, in spite of Jasper's bad reputation and his own doubts:

> CHARLIE: I can't trust anything—liquor, cigarettes. God knows what'll happen when I have sex. At this rate my dick'll probably fall off halfway through. (p. 11)

Charlie also has a close friend, the comically courageous cricket-tragic Jeffrey Lu, the son of refugees from Vietnam. (One of the other major events of 1965 was Doug Walters' test debut, about which Jeffrey is obsessed.) Their friendship is expressed in a series of cheerfully insulting interchanges that provide much of the play's humour.

One of these is their argument about superheroes, when Charlie is arguing that the mortal Batman obviously has more courage than the invulnerable Superman (pp.14-16). Soon after that they meet Laura's sister Eliza, whom Charlie has a crush on but dare not approach; and then the town bully, Warwick, whose size, strength and attendant goons make it easy to be tough. We admire Jeffrey's clownish bravery, as he faces up to these thugs who are thwarting his attempts to get a place in the cricket team. For all Charlie's pathological fear of insects and his general book-nerd gentleness, we admire his courage as he sticks by Jasper. But in the end we discover that it is Laura who has had to endure the most.

Jeffrey teases Charlie about his infatuation with Eliza ('Sassytime!'). Charlie and Eliza's relationship is a beautifully written first-love story, full of awkwardness, misunderstanding and growing tenderness. It is the awkwardness and misunderstanding that obscures another issue of trust, when we finally learn the truth of what they have been inadvertently keeping from each other.

The fifth teenager is of course the dead Laura. In the novel Charlie is haunted by memories and stories of her. In a play he can be haunted by her ghost. It is one of the many brilliant things about Kate Mulvany's adaptation that she brings Laura on stage in the flesh. Laura visits him in his room while he is sleeping. It is she who points out to him the word 'Sorry' scratched on the tree from which she was found hanging, and later on the old car—such a significant relic of Jasper's unknown past—in Mad Jack Lionel's yard. She visits the Lu's house when the vandals trash their beautiful flower garden. Having her so present in Charlie's journey is very moving.

Another theme explored in the play is the idea of the normal and what lies beneath that banal word. When Charlie and Jasper first come back from the terrible scene of the death everything at first seems ordinary again. The town of Corrigan reacts to Laura's disappearance with fear and anxiety and the young people are locked up, as might be expected, but the novel and the play evoke small-town normalcy—the streets, the cricket ground, the pub, the railway, the river, the farmlands and the bushland beyond. It is a portrait of a usually quiet community that is suddenly disrupted, like when your country fights an overseas war and sends your young men off to die, or when you drop the body of a hanged girl into the dark waters of a dam.

Mulvany has also given to Charlie's troubled angry mother, Mrs Bucktin, a wonderful speech in which she reveals all her despair about having to live in such a 'normal' country town.

> MRS BUCKTIN: I reckon it's set in a town of never-ending fucking silence. Silence and space. Dead paddocks and dried-up dams and a bunch of ghosts covered in dust walking around a place where nothing ever changes. It just doesn't fucking change. Stinking men and bored women and incessant heat and filthy flies and fucking on a back seat. Just to feel something, just to feel anything, just to escape the silence. (p.66)

And what is most shocking of all is our realisation at the end of the play that what has happened to Laura is in fact, no matter how outraged we might be, all too normal.

Then there are the adults who control the teenagers' lives, but whom Charlie, as he grows to some sort of early maturity, gradually realises have troubles and secrets of their own. Most of them do not appear (in fact, the only parents who appear on stage are Charlie's), but are looming presences in the story. His mother's own desperation emerges as a reason for her erratic behaviour. His gently quiescent father—who has given him his love of the books which are the solace of his young life and his point of contact with Eliza—teaches him a lot, but is excluded from his secret. Mr Bucktin himself displays great courage when he confronts the gang who are tormenting Jeffrey's father.

Jeffrey's parents are decent, hard-working, refugee immigrants, facing the hostility, and occasionally the friendship, of the people of Corrigan. In his supreme self-confidence, his cheerful acceptance of all the shit thrown at him by Warwick and his mates, and in his energetic wit and cleverness, Jeffrey becomes a defiant trickster figure whose triumph in the iconic Aussie cricket match is one of the great pleasures of the story.

Jasper's violently drunken father only returns to town from time to time to beat up his son. Jasper's Aboriginal mother is long gone, and we eventually find out why and where. This is the source of his fierce independence, and the reason why he has his secret place. He is a teenager who needs somewhere to live and survive on his own. This is why, when Laura turns up dead in his special place, he enlists Charlie to help and their trusting friendship begins.

Eliza and Laura's father and mother are supposedly pillars of the community but the revelation at the end demonstrates how alone these children are. Normal life can be a nightmare.

The other adult is Mad Jack Lionel, the supposedly evil killer of a young woman. He lives isolated on the edge of town, a source of mystery, feared and loathed by all the young people. Stealing from his peach tree has become a rite of passage for tough boys trying to prove their machismo. Jasper's personal relationship to Mad Jack, eventually revealed, and Charlie's understanding of this and his final complicity in the splendid peach tree scene, is one the happiest arcs of the story.

But there remains, as we watch these events, the central question: what happened to Laura? This is the tragic arc of the story, in which most of the questions raised about trust and courage are answered.

Mulvany has taken a novel based in first-person narrative, relying for its story on discoveries, and turned it into a drama based in the actions of characters. The interactions between Charlie and Jasper, Jeffrey and Eliza are brought concisely and gloriously to theatrical life. She takes Charlie's painfully introspective library research into the violent crimes with which he becomes obsessed, and gives the story of the torture of Sylvia Likens (p.29) to Eliza to tell to Charlie. This raises the stakes for Eliza and gives the actor something very strong to play:

> 'The sister. Jenny. Why didn't she tell someone at school? A neighbour? Anyone? She was Sylvia's only ally and she didn't say a word. Why would she do that?' (p.29)

In this exchange neither of them knows that the other knows the truth about Laura, and we, the audience, don't know that Eliza knows what happened to Laura. It makes for a rich subtext.

There are many such scenes of complex dramatic irony. When Charlie has his warm scene with his father and asks if he can join in the search for Laura, Mr Bucktin says they might find something that 'might not be for eyes of children' (p.35). We know that Charlie knows that they will not find anything, that his eyes have already seen more, and that his hands have done something about it.

Kate Mulvany has taken from Silvey's novel the deceptively simple but moving final refrain that the young Charlie reiterates so powerfully and with such a sense of innocent shock, surprise and outrage, as if he cannot believe that this is the way things go in the world. Here he shares it with Eliza, as we learn the truth at last.

'This is what happened ...'

John McCallum
Sydney, 2017

John McCallum is a theatre reviewer for *The Australian*.

Jasper Jones was first presented by Barking Gecko Theatre Company at Studio Underground, State Theatre Centre of WA, Perth, on 17 July 2014, with the following cast:

JASPER JONES	Shaka Cook
CHARLIE BUCKTIN	James Beck
JEFFREY LU	Hoa Xuande
MRS BUCKTIN	Alexandra Jones
ELIZA WISHART / LAURA WISHART	Elizabeth Blackmore
MAD JACK LIONEL / MR BUCKTIN	Humphrey Bower

Director, John Sheedy
Set & Costume Designer, Michael Scott-Mitchell
Lighting Designer, Trent Suidgeest
Sound Designer, Ben Collins

CHARACTERS

CHARLIE BUCKTIN, a bookish white 14-year-old boy
JASPER JONES, an Indigenous 16-year-old boy
LAURA WISHART, a dead 15-year-old girl
ELIZA WISHART, Laura's mysterious 14-year-old sister
JEFFREY LU, Charlie's Vietnamese next-door neighbour, best friend
    and cricket fanatic
MR BUCKTIN, Charlie's father
MRS BUCKTIN, Charlie's mother
MAD JACK LIONEL, the scariest bloke in town
WARWICK TRENT, town bully
CLARRY, Warwick Trent's henchman
OFFICER, philanderer
MRS LU, Jeffrey's mother (voice only)
STRANGER, a way out
MOB, faceless citizens
MEN, brutal coppers

This play is ideally for seven performers, but can be done with six.
The doubling for six works best as:

CHARLIE
JASPER
LAURA / ELIZA / MEN / MOB
JEFFREY / STRANGER / MEN / MOB
MRS BUCKTIN / WARWICK / MEN
MR BUCKTIN / CLARRY / OFFICER / MAD JACK / MOB

With seven performers, MAD JACK can be played as a single character.
Mrs Lu's voice can be pre-recorded.

SETTING

The (fictional) West Australian town of Corrigan during the summer
of 1965.

ACT ONE

SCENE ONE

On a dark stage, beneath a tree, the louvred window of a sleep-out is illuminated by the dim glow of a kerosene lamp. Inside the room is a thirteen-year-old boy, CHARLIE BUCKTIN, *reading a book intently in his glasses and pyjamas.*

The only sound is the cricking of summer cicadas.

Then …

A dark creeping figure makes its way deftly, silently across the space to Charlie's window.

CHARLIE *does not look up from his book.*

A beat.

The figure looks around, then … raps abruptly on the louvred window.

CHARLIE *gasps and falls out of bed with a fright. He looks in amazement at his visitor, then turns to us …*

CHARLIE: [*whispering*] Jasper Jones has come to my window!

JASPER: [*whispering*] Charlie! Charlie, come out here.

CHARLIE: He knows my name! Wow! [*To* JASPER] What are you doing here?

JASPER: I need your help, Charlie. Come out.

CHARLIE: It's really late, Jasper. My parents might wake up—

JASPER: Charlie. Hurry up. I need you.

> *A beat.*

CHARLIE: [*to us*] Jasper Jones needs *me?!*

> CHARLIE *removes the slats of his window and peers around fearfully as* JASPER *waits outside.* CHARLIE *squeezes awkwardly through the window—all arse and pyjamas. He splats heavily to the ground then gets up quickly, pretending it never happened.*

JASPER: You right?

CHARLIE: Yep.

JASPER: You ready?

CHARLIE: For what?

JASPER: I tole you, Charlie. I need your help. Come on. We gotta go.

> JASPER *starts to walk away.* CHARLIE *hesitates.*

CHARLIE: Hang on.

> CHARLIE *leans in through his window. He fishes out a pair of ridiculously chunky sandals and puts them on. He is now wearing pyjamas with the dumbest pair of sandals ever seen on a pair of feet.*

In case there's doublegees.

JASPER: Come on. We gotta hurry.

> *As they walk,* CHARLIE *speaks to us once more.*

CHARLIE: You have to understand, I've never snuck out before. I'm a virgin to this kind of thing. Actually, I'm pretty much a virgin to *every* kind of thing. Except books. So me sneaking out with Jasper Jones, who is known throughout Corrigan as the worst kid in town, well, it's fair to say this is particularly out of character for me.

JASPER: Keep up, Charlie.

CHARLIE: [*to us*] In this town, Jasper is the first to be blamed for everything. Whatever the misdemeanour—nicking lollies from the store, throwing lit matches down the mines, or sneaking through fences to push over cows—no matter how clear their own child is guilty, parents ask immediately, 'Were you with that motherless half-caste Jasper Jones?'

JASPER: Quick, mate.

CHARLIE: [*to us*] And the kids always nod, because Jasper's involvement instantly absolves them. Their parents think their poor little child has somehow been momentarily led astray. And so the case is closed with just one simple instruction, 'Stay away from Jasper Jones'.

JASPER: Hurry up, Charlie. We gotta hurry.

CHARLIE: [*to us*] So me being here, under a full moon, being led by Jasper Jones past the brown lawns and gardens of my sleeping neighbourhood, past the cricket pitch, past the railway, past the power station, over the bridge, through the farm district, and knowing what my mother would do if she found out where I was … Well, let's just say this is something *way* more adventurous than anything Huckleberry Finn ever did.

JASPER *offers* CHARLIE *a cigarette.*

JASPER: Wanna smoke?

A beat. CHARLIE *looks uncomfortable.*

CHARLIE: Oh, nah …
JASPER: You sure?
CHARLIE: Yeah …
JASPER: I didn't nick 'em from the shop, if that's what you're worried about.
CHARLIE: Oh … that's good.
JASPER: I nicked 'em from me old man.

CHARLIE *rubs his belly.*

CHARLIE: It … it's just that I've smoked so many tonight I'm already full.

JASPER *turns to a doorway near a tree branch that is bursting with peaches.*

CHARLIE *gasps.*

Wh-what are we doing here?

JASPER *stares at the doorway.*

Jasper … This is … This is Mad Jack Lionel's place.

A beat.

We really … *really* shouldn't be here.

JASPER *keeps staring at the door.*

Are you gonna steal a peach? Is that why we're here?

JASPER *still doesn't answer.*

CHARLIE *turns to us again.*

No kid in Corrigan has actually ever laid eyes on Mad Jack Lionel. But we've heard all about him from our parents. He lives in that house there and hasn't stepped outside of it since he killed a young woman a long time ago.

He indicates the branch full of peaches.

A popular test of courage in Corrigan is to nick a peach from the tree of Mad Jack Lionel. After you've eaten it, the stone of the peach is kept as a souvenir of your heroics and is universally admired and envied. It's guaranteed to earn you at least a month of respect at school.

He gazes admiringly at the peaches.

However, as much as I like the idea of raising my station in this town, I was unfortunately born without speed or courage, which are both essential to the stealing of Mad Jack Lionel's peaches.

JASPER: We're not here to steal a peach.

CHARLIE: [*to us*] Phew. / [*To* JASPER] Do … do you reckon it's all true, Jasper? What they say about him?

JASPER: Most people around here talk a lot of bullshit, but I reckon they're on the money with that one. He's mad alright.

He spits on the dirt.

CHARLIE: Fersure.

He spits too—pissily.

Completely.

JASPER: I seen him, you know. A bunch of times.

CHARLIE: Really? When? How?

But JASPER *just flicks his cigarette at Mad Jack's place and starts walking again.* CHARLIE *hurries after him.*

Is he tall? I heard he's about eight feet high and four feet wide. Does he really have a scar down his face? Does he really have a glass eye that follows you wherever you go? And a tattoo of a skull and crossbones on his arm? Does he really smell like wee? What's his voice like? Raspy? Croaky? What? Does his hair really come all the way down to his knees? And did he really make a pact with the devil? I heard that once. Jasper? Jasper?

He trips over and hurries back to his feet again.

JASPER: Come on, Charlie. We're close now. Hurry.

CHARLIE: [*to us*] This is, by far, my worst transgression. Probably my only ever transgression. But I follow Jasper on. Branches and shrubs snap

back at me. The river disappears then reappears again. The paperbarks
and floodgums look like they want to snatch us up and then …

JASPER: We're here.

They stop walking.

I can trust you, Charlie, can't I?

CHARLIE: I reckon. Yeah.

JASPER: It's through here.

CHARLIE: What is?

JASPER puts a hand on CHARLIE's shoulder.

JASPER: I'm really sorry, mate.

CHARLIE: Huh? For what?

A long moment. JASPER stares at CHARLIE intently.

JASPER: This.

JASPER reveals …

SCENE TWO

*Hanging at the end of a long noose, a young girl in a white nightdress.
Like a still ghost in the darkness. Her face is bruised and bloodied. Her
long hair is loose. Her head is held at a strange angle as she seems to
gaze down at the boys.*

CHARLIE screams suddenly but JASPER covers his mouth with his hand.

*CHARLIE struggles to get away, his eyes never leaving the girl, but JASPER
is too strong for him.*

*Finally, CHARLIE gives up in exhaustion and JASPER removes his hand
from his mouth.*

CHARLIE: Who is that?

JASPER: It's Laura Wishart.

Silence. The two boys watch LAURA hanging.

I bin away for a while, Charlie. Outta town. I came back here tonight
and the first thing I saw was Laura. Up there. I grabbed her legs and
tried to hold her up. Tried to save her. But she was gone already. I dint
know what to do. So I ran to your place and knocked on your window.

Panic hits CHARLIE.

CHARLIE: Jasper, I shouldn't be here! I have to go back home! You have to tell someone about this!

JASPER: I can't do that.

CHARLIE: I don't understand. What happened? *Why would she do that?!*

JASPER: She dint do it, Charlie. She can't have. You see that rope? That's *my* rope. I use it to swing over the dam. But I always hide it after—I wrap it around that branch so no-one can see it. Cos this is *my* place. This is where I spend most of my time. It's *my* place.

CHARLIE: Well, she must have found it when she shinnied up the tree.

JASPER: She couldn't have shinnied up the tree, Charlie. Laura … she's a lady. She's delicate, you know. She couldn't have done it herself. And look up there. Look at her face.

CHARLIE: I don't want to.

JASPER: *Look,* Charlie.

CHARLIE *does, reluctantly.*

Someone's beaten her up. The same someone that strung her up that tree, I reckon.

CHARLIE: But who? Who in Corrigan would do that?

He looks terrified.

Was it … was it *you?*

A beat.

JASPER *stares at* CHARLIE.

CHARLIE *goes to run but* JASPER *stops him.*

JASPER: Charlie, I promise you, mate—I dint do this.

CHARLIE *settles a little but then panics again. He whispers, afraid.*

CHARLIE: Shit, Jasper! What if whoever did this is still here? Watching us!

JASPER: There's no-one here. I can tell.

CHARLIE: How can you tell?

JASPER: I just can.

A beat.

We gotta find out who did this, Charlie. We gotta find out who killed Laura.

CHARLIE: No we don't! We go to the police and we tell them everything you just told me. They'll find who did it. That's their job, Jasper!
JASPER: Nah. This is somethin' *we* gotta do.
CHARLIE: We can't solve a murder! I'm fourteen! You're … Wait, how old are you?
JASPER: Not sure. Sixteen. I think.
CHARLIE: We can't solve a murder! We gotta get the cops. We gotta tell our parents.
JASPER: Bloody hell, Charlie, you just don't get it, do you? We can't tell *anyone. Especially* the coppers. Because they'll come here, see it's my place, see her face, see my rope and they'll say it's me that did this.
CHARLIE: That's bullshit, Jasper. They won't think that.
JASPER: Really? And what was the first thing *you* thought?

> CHARLIE *looks distraught as he glances again at* LAURA *'s hanging body.* JASPER *speaks to him calmly.*

This town thinks I'm an animal, Charlie. They think I belong in a cage and now here's the perfect chance for them to do just that. And it'll get even worse once I'm in there. You know what they do to fellas like me in prison?

> *A beat.*

We need to get her down from there. We need to get her down and hide her till we find out who did this.
CHARLIE: But her poor family. They should know what's happened.
JASPER: They will know. Soon enough. Everything's gonna be orright, Charlie. You just gotta get brave, like me. I'd never let you get in trouble. Promise.
CHARLIE: Where *are* we gonna put her?
JASPER: The dam, mate. We're gonna put her in the dam.

> *He goes to* LAURA *in the noose.*

Hold her, Charlie. *Hold her!*

> CHARLIE *does, reluctantly.*

CHARLIE: She's still warm!
JASPER: I know.
CHARLIE: It's only just happened!

JASPER: I know. Now hurry. Get her down.
CHARLIE: But she's still warm!
JASPER: Charlie, come on. Please.

They start to lower her gently.

Now get this fucken rope off her neck.
CHARLIE: The knot's too tight!
JASPER: Hold her hair back, Charlie.
CHARLIE: She's bleeding. She's bleeding. She's bleeding.

JASPER *removes the rope.*

JASPER: I got her.
CHARLIE: Please take her. Please take her. Please take her.

CHARLIE *and* JASPER *leap back in shock.*

[*To us*] I wasn't expecting the deep, dark wounds around Laura's neck.

JASPER *moves back to* LAURA. *He checks the skin on her arms, her face, her legs. He inspects every bruise, every wound, delicately, lovingly, as he aligns her body on the ground.*

JASPER: Turn around, Charlie.
CHARLIE: Why?
JASPER: I need to check something else.
CHARLIE: What?
JASPER: Just turn around.

CHARLIE *does.*

Slowly, JASPER *lifts the hem of Laura's dress. He stares beneath it solemnly for a moment then turns his head away. He stands slowly, then disappears into the tree.*

CHARLIE *turns to see* JASPER *has gone. It is just him alone with the dead girl.*

CHARLIE: Jasper?

Silence.

CHARLIE *walks slowly toward* LAURA.

He stands over her.

He crouches beside her. He reaches out a hand and touches her.

He pulls back in shock.

Then ... he reaches out again and feels her skin.

JASPER *appears suddenly, with an armful of stones.*

JASPER: Charlie. Help me get her in.

CHARLIE: But Jasper ...

JASPER: Charlie. Come on. You gotta get brave. Help me get her in.

CHARLIE *reluctantly assists* JASPER *with* LAURA*'s body.*

As they get to the edge of the dam ...

Ready, Charlie?

CHARLIE *looks anything but ready.*

One ... two ...

Blackout.

Silence.

In the darkness ...

CHARLIE: [*to us*] We have drowned the dead.

SCENE THREE

Lights up.

LAURA *is gone.*

JASPER *drops to his knees and stares at the dam.*

CHARLIE *watches on, wide-eyed.*

JASPER *gets a bottle out of his trousers. Swigs it. Sits on the ground and swigs it again. Offers it to* CHARLIE.

CHARLIE: Oh, nah ...

JASPER: You sure?

CHARLIE: Yeah ...

JASPER *drinks.*

What is it?

JASPER: The old man's favourite. Bushmills. Tastes like piss and oil.

CHARLIE: Won't he get cross that you nicked it?

JASPER: He's always cross. Useless fuckin' whitefella. Wish he'd get sent off to Vietnam. Give me some fuckin' peace. Here.

CHARLIE *has a drink. He gags.*

You right, mate?

CHARLIE: Yeah. Just … went down the wrong hole …

A beat. CHARLIE *regains his composure.*

Jasper … how did you even know someone like Laura?

JASPER *takes another swig.*

JASPER: Laura was the *only* person I ever felt like I knew. Rest of the town reckons I'm trouble. A filthy thieving half-caste.

CHARLIE: My dad doesn't let me use that word.

JASPER: Half-caste? Really? Good on ya, Charlie. I knew I picked the right fella to help me.

CHARLIE: Why did you pick me? You've never even spoken to me before. You don't even go to my school.

JASPER: I don't go to any school.

A beat.

I just seen you, Charlie. Around town. Always with your head in a book. Quiet. Polite. Serious. Seems to me you're a bit of a thinker. You're different to the rest of this town.

CHARLIE: I am?

JASPER *takes another swig.* CHARLIE *does too. It goes down a little better this time.*

I am.

JASPER: And Laura liked you too.

CHARLIE: She did?

JASPER: She did.

A beat.

She was real smart like that. She was like my mum and my family all at the same time, you know? Real funny. Real clever. We never fooled around either. Not much, anyway. We made a promise to each other, Laura and me, that we'd move to the city as soon as we could. Get out of Corrigan. Make millions.

His smile fades. They drink again.

CHARLIE: Did you used to bring her here, Jasper?

JASPER: I did. A lot. But always a different way through the bush so she'd never be able to get here on her own. Cos this is my place, Charlie. And I only wanted her here if I was by her side.

He takes another swig. CHARLIE *takes two.*

And that's why I reckon someone's trying to set me up. Someone's follered me here and knows it's my place. And they've killed Laura and want me to take the blame, like I always do. And who kills women in this town? Mad Jack Lionel, that's fuckin' who.

Silence. They stare at the dam.

CHARLIE: Hey, Jasper … I reckon I'm ready for a cigarette now.

JASPER grins and holds out the packet of ciggies. CHARLIE *puts a cigarette in his mouth and leans in to* JASPER*'s match.* JASPER *draws the flame away and flips the cigarette the right way round in* CHARLIE*'s mouth.*

CHARLIE inhales deeply and coughs like a drain.

The cigarette falls down his shirt.

A comedy of errors ensues as CHARLIE *dances around the dam, swatting at the cigarette, coughing up a lung and burning himself.*

He coughs so much he starts retching. JASPER *slaps him on the back as he crawls around the floor, retching. He lifts his head drunkenly.*

I can't trust anything—liquor, cigarettes. God knows what'll happen when I have sex. At this rate my dick'll probably fall off halfway through.

JASPER laughs at this. He laughs and laughs. He laughs so much he starts retching too. CHARLIE *looks shocked.*

I thought you could hold your liquor!

JASPER: Yeah, I can. Just not for long.

JASPER crawls over to the dam. Over his shoulder …

Thank you, Charlie.

A beat.

We gotta find out who did this.

He returns his attention to the still water of the dam. He kisses his own hand and places it in the water—sending love to LAURA—*before passing out.*

CHARLIE *is still laying on the ground nearby.*

CHARLIE: [*to us*] Earlier tonight I was a fourteen-year-old kid about to start my summer holidays with my head buried in a Mark Twain novel. Now ... now I've absconded from my house, I stink of cigarettes, I'm drunk, and I just threw a dead girl in a dam.

A beat.

A warm light starts to fill the stage.

CHARLIE *grabs a blanket from inside the tree and covers* JASPER *with it.*

He takes one last look into the dam and waves sadly.

As he travels hurriedly ...

I want to invite Jasper with me. Take him home, give him my bed and a nice cool bath and a good book to read. But I can't. Because that's not how Corrigan works.

He arrives home. He removes his sandals, climbs in his window and replaces the slats. He looks around in silence.

A beat.

But now I'm here, back in the safety of my sleep-out, I realise everything's changed anyway. My room doesn't feel like mine anymore. It's like ... somehow ... the universe shifted when Laura left it, and the splash as we lowered her into the dam has already rippled across the town.

He lays down in bed.

Pretty soon Corrigan will start demanding answers as to what happened tonight. The coppers will come and start asking questions about Laura Wishart. Everyone will start looking for someone to blame. I've read enough books to know that. They'll come soon. They will.

A beat.

I just hope they don't blame me.

Lights down.

SCENE FOUR

The sound of a cricket match.

*Lights up on a Vietnamese boy—*JEFFREY*—waiting beside a colourful, manicured, floral garden. He sits beside a radio and looks impatient as he sips a tall drink. The radio plays Normie Rowe's 1960s hit song 'Que Será Será'.*

CHARLIE *appears.*

JEFFREY: Where have you *been?* You're such an *idiot!* I knocked on your door *five times.* That means I had to speak to your mum *five times.* God, Charlie! Do you even know what *day* it is?

CHARLIE: I slept in. Took me a while to drop off last night. It was … hot.

 He changes the subject.

Your dad's flowers look nice.

JEFFREY: Thanks. They're Queen Elizabeth's Roses.

CHARLIE: What? Does she own them?

JEFFREY: Probably. She owns everything, doesn't she?

 A beat.

CHARLIE: Hey, are they your mum's lychee balls?

 He fishes around in JEFFREY*'s drink.*

What day *is* it?

 JEFFREY *sighs and starts gathering his things—a cricket bat, ball, backpack …*

JEFFREY: What *day* is it? Are you *joking*?! It's Dougie Walters' debut, Charlie! First Ashes Test of 1965! I got high hopes for this one, Charlie. He's gonna be *huge.* Come on. Let's go.

 He calls inside the house.

Mum! We're going into town to play some fuckin' cricket!

MRS LU'S VOICE: Okay, dahling.

CHARLIE: Did you just swear at your mum?

JEFFREY: It's okay. She doesn't understand swear words. Look.

 He calls again.

Mum! Charlie loves your fuckin' lychee balls!

He grins at CHARLIE.

Do you hear me, Mum? Charlie really fuckin' loves balls!

MRS LU'S VOICE: Okay! Thass good! Thank you, Chully! Bye-bye, dah-lings.

The two boys stifle their giggles. JEFFREY *starts to walk ...*

CHARLIE: Don't you wanna listen to the game?

JEFFREY: It's been delayed. Pissing down over there. Bloody Brisbane. They should just play the matches here. No fear of it getting rained out in Corrigan.

A beat.

Spiderman, on the other hand, well, he'd be useless in this town.

As they travel, JEFFREY *shows exceptional prowess with the bat and ball. Miming drives, taking catches, rubbing the ball hard on his groin ...*

CHARLIE: How do you figure that?

JEFFREY: He's only useful in an urban environment. He needs things to swing between, otherwise he's just a weird-looking guy with snot shooting out of his wrists.

CHARLIE: Fair point.

JEFFREY: And that's why Superman is the superior superhero. He's all-terrain. Simple.

CHARLIE: Superman is boring. He's too accomplished. There's no effort with him. No character. The only drama comes from a chance meeting with some kryptonite. His only weakness is some arbitrary green mineral.

JEFFREY: You are such a fucking communist, Charlie. He has other weaknesses beside kryptonite.

CHARLIE: Yeah? Name one.

JEFFREY: Love, dickhead. Love. His family. Lois Lane. He loves them. And that love can be endangered and used against him.

CHARLIE: Lois Lane. Pfft.

JEFFREY: Queer.

He polishes his ball.

CHARLIE: I'm not queer. You're the one rubbing leather on your dick.

JEFFREY: Well, who do you reckon, then? Greatest superhero. Go.

CHARLIE: Batman.
JEFFREY: *Batman?!*

>   *He cracks up.*

Charlie, you're *such* an *idiot*!
CHARLIE: You're an idiot.
JEFFREY: You're an imbecile.
CHARLIE: You're an *ignoramus*.

>   JEFFREY *is exasperated.*

JEFFREY: Batman is just an eccentric billionaire with insomnia. He has a cool car and a handy belt but he doesn't have any super*powers*. He's not super*human*. He's not super*anything*. Therefore he can't be a super*hero*.

CHARLIE: You're super*delusional*, my little Vietnamese friend. The definition of super is 'greater than usual'. So in every aspect—money, mansion, car, belt—Batman is indeed *super*. Added to this, he has an alter ego, he has a costume, he fights for Truth and Justice, he has arch enemies, and he does it without any weird mutations like the other 'superheroes'. He's just a really determined guy. He's normal. In him we see ourselves. And that's what makes him the best. To be Batman takes a lot of courage.

JEFFREY: Are you *joking*?! Superman *invented* courage. He steps in front of bullets.

CHARLIE: Of course he does. He's *invulnerable*. If you know a bullet can't possibly hurt you then it's not that brave to stand in front of it, is it?

>   JEFFREY *is at a loss to answer.*

Batman is mortal. His life is at risk with every battle. The more you have to lose, the braver you are for standing up. That's why Batman is superior to Superman and that's why I am superior to you in this argument.

JEFFREY: Careful, Chuck, or I will be forced to pull out my infamous Bruce Lee one-inch punch—a fierce concentration of energy toward a single point in the body that can be released in a moment of explosive power. A technique that is so powerful that a fist can pass right through a man's heart.

He crouches, his fist out in front, spasming slightly with kinetic energy, emitting a low Bruce Lee-style growl. CHARLIE *shakes his head—he's seen this before.*

Suddenly—

Whooooooooo! Sassytime!

JEFFREY *drops his stance.*

A teenage girl has appeared. She holds a book. At first, it is like the ghost of LAURA *has appeared and* CHARLIE *looks momentarily dumbstruck as he stares at her.*

ELIZA: Hello, Charlie. Hello, Jeffrey.

A beat. JEFFREY *shrugs at* ELIZA *nonchalantly.* CHARLIE *gapes at her, then turns to us …*

CHARLIE: Eliza Wishart. Laura's little sister. It's like looking at a ghost. I can't believe Eliza is just wandering around Corrigan when her sister is at the bottom of the dam. But then I remember, the Wisharts don't know that yet. They probably haven't checked her room. They probably haven't seen that her bed hasn't been slept in for hours and hours. They probably …

CHARLIE *turns back to* ELIZA *and gulps like a fish catching its breath.*

JEFFREY: Charlie?

CHARLIE *turns back to us …*

CHARLIE: I wanna tell Eliza everything. What I saw. What I did. I want to assure her Jasper Jones didn't do that to her sister. And I want to hold Eliza as she cries and find all the right words to say to her.

JEFFREY: Charlie? You right?

CHARLIE *is still stammering silently as he stares at* ELIZA. *He points to her book—Harper Lee's* To Kill a Mockingbird.

CHARLIE: That's … a bood gook.

ELIZA *looks at* CHARLIE *strangely. He tries again.*

A googa booga. A … goo … A goo … A goo …

He looks panicked. The words just won't come.

A goo … A boo … A gooboogoo …

Finally ...

A good ... book.

ELIZA *smiles.*

ELIZA: Yes. It is.

A young man, WARWICK, *arrives in cricket gear, with his mate,* CLARRY. WARWICK *leers at* ELIZA.

WARWICK: Oi, Wishart. Show us your tits.

CLARRY *chuckles.* ELIZA *glares for a moment at* WARWICK. CHARLIE *ducks his head nervously.* JEFFREY *starts swinging his bat cockily.*

ELIZA: [*as she departs*] Goodbye, Charlie. Goodbye, Jeffrey.

ELIZA *settles under the tree nearby and reads her book.*

JEFFREY *shifts excitedly in front of* WARWICK.

JEFFREY: Reckon I might get a bowl in today, Warwick? Whaddaya reckon?

WARWICK: Fuck off, cunt eyes.

CLARRY *chuckles.* JEFFREY *is not dissuaded. He just wants a bowl.*

JEFFREY: I reckon I've perfected my left-arm orthodox. Got a nice spin to it. I'd love to try it out in the nets.

WARWICK: I said fuck off, Cong.

CLARRY *chuckles.*

JEFFREY: Got a new ball and everything. Been saving up for it for a year. Check it out.

He shows WARWICK *the ball.* WARWICK *takes it and hurls it.* CLARRY *chuckles.*

Nice throw, Warwick! I'll get it!

He runs to retrieve the ball.

WARWICK *glares at* CHARLIE, *who swallows fearfully.*

CHARLIE: [*to us*] Warwick Trent holds the record for the most peaches stolen from the tree of Mad Jack Lionel. He's got four pits in his pocket from four separate occasions. He's had real, actual sex. More than once. He's been in more fights than anyone and won all of them—

including one with Trevor Maloney—a toothless miner. Warwick is feared and revered and I hate him like poison. [*To* WARWICK, *friendly*] Hallo, Warwick. How are you today?

WARWICK *keeps glaring at* CHARLIE.

CHARLIE *returns to us.*

[*To us*] I have to be careful not to use big words with Warwick because it makes him mad. If I use a word in class that has too many syllables, like, say, 'monosyllabic', Warwick and his henchmen will seek me out after school and repeat the offending word as they beat seven shades of shit out of me.

WARWICK *'s ears prick.*

WARWICK: Whaddya say, queer?
CHARLIE: Mono … syll … abic?

WARWICK *punches* CHARLIE *in the shoulder and mocks him.*

WARWICK: Mono … syll … abic.

CLARRY *chuckles.* WARWICK *punches* CHARLIE *again.*

Mono … syll … abic.

CLARRY *chuckles.* WARWICK *punches* CHARLIE *again.*

Mono … syll … abic.

CLARRY *chuckles.* WARWICK *punches* CHARLIE *again. As the beating continues,* CHARLIE *turns to us once more.*

CHARLIE: The fact is, Warwick shouldn't even be in my class but he also holds the record for the most grades repeated. Three. So I'm stuck with him till at least *I* graduate.

JEFFREY *runs back with the ball.*

JEFFREY: So what do you reckon, Warwick? Maybe I'll get a go in the nets today?

WARWICK *throws the ball again.* CLARRY *chuckles.* JEFFREY *grins, unperturbed.*

Nice chuck, Warwick! I'll get it!

JEFFREY *runs off again.* WARWICK *begins hitting* CHARLIE *again.*

WARWICK: Mono … syll … abic.

  CLARRY *chuckles.* WARWICK *punches* CHARLIE *again.*

Mono … syll … abic.

  CLARRY *chuckles.* WARWICK *punches* CHARLIE *again.*

Mono … syll … abic.

  And so it continues on …

CHARLIE: [*to us*] Every now and then the Country Week boys will let Jeffrey pad up. Then they take bets on body hits and they bowl as short and fast as they possibly can. Every time they hit him, they exchange money. Even the coach gets in on it. It's horrible to watch, but Jeffrey never gives in. He's completely impervious to their taunts. I guess he's been through worse. When he cuts in for a bowl, though, that's where he shines. It's a thing of beauty.

  JEFFREY *returns. His confidence is as strong as ever.*

JEFFREY: So what do you reckon, Warwick? Can I have a go today?

  WARWICK *stops punching* CHARLIE *and considers* JEFFREY.

WARWICK: One bowl, slapface. One bowl.

  He gives the bat to CHARLIE.

Here. You bat.

CHARLIE: Jeffrey, we can just play on our street. Let's go home.

WARWICK: I said you bat.

  CHARLIE *reluctantly takes the bat from* WARWICK, *aware that* ELIZA *is now watching from beneath the tree. He weakly assumes a batting position.* JEFFREY *walks excitedly to his mark, rubbing his ball on his groin the whole time.* WARWICK *whispers to* CLARRY.

  A chant starts from the other players: 'Cong, Cong, Cong, Cong, Cong!'

  As JEFFREY *bowls,* CHARLIE *screams and ducks fearfully.*

  WARWICK *pulls down* JEFFREY'*s pants.* CLARRY *pulls down* CHARLIE'*s. They run off laughing toward the other players.*

Ha! Fuckin' queers!

CLARRY: Fuckin' queers!

WARWICK: Fuckin' queers!

> CHARLIE *and* JEFFREY *are left standing with their pants down.* ELIZA *watches from afar.* JEFFREY *beams.*

JEFFREY: Did you see the spin on that bewdie?

> CHARLIE *pulls his pants up, mortified.*

CHARLIE: I can't believe we fell for that.

JEFFREY: I mean, even Dougie Walters couldn't have hit that ball. That was a corker!

CHARLIE: Jeffrey, would you pull your pants up, please? They're still laughing at us.

JEFFREY: Float like a butterfly, sting like a bee. Your bat can't hit what your eyes can't see! *I am the greatest!*

CHARLIE: You're standing on a cricket pitch with your pants down while the whole Country Week team laughs at you. Why didn't you pull out your one-inch punch?

JEFFREY: I don't need murder on my hands, my friend. I'll reserve it for those who truly deserve it. Besides, if nobody had stolen Muhammad Ali's bike, he would never have hit anyone. Bring it on!

> *He finally pulls his pants up.*

> ELIZA *stands, brushes off her dress and leaves.*

> CHARLIE *looks demoralised.*

CHARLIE: Jeffrey, let's go home.

> *They start to travel. As they do,* JEFFREY *plays cricket shots all the way home and the light turns to dusk.*

> CHARLIE *turns to us …*

From behind, Eliza looks exactly like her sister. I wonder how Laura's going down there on the bottom of the dam. Her fingers and toes would be really wrinkly by now, like when you have a long bath. Then again, maybe she doesn't have fingers and toes anymore. Maybe the yabbies have eaten them all away.

SCENE FIVE

They have reached Charlie's house. A light shines in a study and the silhouette of a man can be seen sitting inside.

JEFFREY: What does your dad *do* in there all night?
CHARLIE: I dunno. Hides.
JEFFREY: From who?

> MRS BUCKTIN *appears, dressed to the nines.* JEFFREY *is suddenly all charm.*

Good evening, Mrs Bucktin!
MRS BUCKTIN: Oh, hello, Jeffrey. [*To* CHARLIE] Hello, Lord Muck. Deigned to grace us with your presence, have you?
CHARLIE: We were playing cricket.
MRS BUCKTIN: Well, Mr Bradman, there's some cold meat in the fridge. I'm going out. Toodle pip.

> *She gestures to her husband's silhouette then wanders off, jangling car keys.*

CHARLIE: Your hair looks pretty, Mum.

> *She turns.*

MRS BUCKTIN: What did you say?
CHARLIE: I said … your hair looks pretty.

> *A beat.*

MRS BUCKTIN: Why would you say that?

> CHARLIE *shrugs.*

CHARLIE: Cos … it does?

> MRS BUCKTIN *stares at the boys.*

MRS BUCKTIN: Well, thank you.

> *She saunters off.*

JEFFREY: I can't tell whether your mum is mean or not.
CHARLIE: My dad says she's got 'droll wit'.
JEFFREY: At least your parents speak English. At my house it's all …

> *He does a rather over-the-top impersonation of his stern father and his shrill mother that leaves them both in stitches.*

'*Jeffrey! Bắt cá hai tay! Bắt cá hai tay!*'
CHARLIE: What does that mean?
JEFFREY: It means, 'Jeffrey! You must catch the fish with two hands! You must catch the fish with two hands!'

CHARLIE: What does *that* mean?
JEFFREY: Buggered if I know. What's wrong with a fishing rod?

A beat. They look again at the window, where MR BUCKTIN *sits.*

CHARLIE: It was supposed to be for my sister, that room.
JEFFREY: What sister?
CHARLIE: My baby sister. She died inside Mum.
JEFFREY: Wow. That's creepy.

A beat.

Does that mean she's still inside her?
CHARLIE: Nah. She still had to give birth to her. Except instead of a live baby it was a dead one.
JEFFREY: Whoa.
CHARLIE: And ever since, my dad goes into that room every night and does whatever it is he does. And Mum goes out and does whatever it is she does.
JEFFREY: Maybe he's writing a book.

CHARLIE *is a little put out.*

CHARLIE: I don't think so. I'm the writer in our family.
JEFFREY: How's the Great Australian Novel going?
CHARLIE: Just waiting for the right subject matter.

A beat.

Jeffrey, did you ever see a dead body?
JEFFREY: [*slightly disappointed*] Nah. Not yet. My parents saw a lot though, I reckon. My dad has weird nightmares about stuff.

A beat.

See you tomorrow?

He starts to leave. CHARLIE *calls out to him.*

CHARLIE: Jeffrey, how would you wanna die? If you could choose.
JEFFREY: I reckon struck by lightning. At the MCG. After retiring on three hundred and thirty-four runs in front of a packed stadium. As I raise my bat, the dark Melbourne clouds break and a single splintering bolt jolts thousands of volts through me. And all that's left is a small, noble pile of ashes inside my box. Which is, of course, indestructible.

And he is gone.

CHARLIE *enters his bedroom and strips down to his singlet as the lights dim. He's lit eerily by his lantern.*

CHARLIE: [*to us*] Last year in Perth, they hanged Eric Edgar Cooke—the Nedlands Monster. He went from house to house in the dark of night, snuck into people's sleep-outs, stabbed them, shot them, strangled them and axed them. When they caught him and asked him why he did it he said, 'I just wanted to hurt somebody'.

A beat.

The weirdest thing is that in a hundred years from now, more or less, everyone in Corrigan, in Australia, in the world, every parent, child, every animal, everyone will have died. Including me. In all sorts of different ways. And I can't stop thinking about that. About Laura. About how she died last night. Was it because someone just wanted to hurt somebody? Does Corrigan have its very own Eric Edgar Cooke? Is it Mad Jack Lionel? And when is the town gonna wake up and realise what's going on?

A beat.

I wish Jasper Jones had never come to my window. But at the same time, more than anything, I wish he'd visit me now …

He peers out of his window, searching.

Then … he yawns deeply before laying down to sleep.

A moment of quiet—the only sound is the crickets chirping.

Then … LAURA WISHART *wanders across the stage, her dress bloody, her hair wet.*

She stands by Charlie's window and peers inside.

She enters Charlie's bedroom.

She stands over him as he sleeps.

She reaches out to touch him.

The chirp of crickets becomes almost deafening.

Blackout.

SCENE SIX

The sound of crickets becomes the nasal thrum of a single wasp.

CHARLIE *opens his eyes.*

Gasps.

He tumbles out of bed and screams as he swats at the wasp wildly.

He runs out of his sleep-out, smack bang into his mother who is sorting through washing.

His father reads a newspaper silently.

CHARLIE *stands awkwardly in front of his parents, wearing only his singlet and shorts.*

MRS BUCKTIN: Charlie, we don't wander willy-nilly half-naked around the house.

CHARLIE: I … I'm just a bit hot today.

MRS BUCKTIN: Of course you're hot. It's Corrigan. It's always bloody hot.

She peers at his legs.

When did you get those?

CHARLIE *is mortified.*

CHARLIE: What?

MRS BUCKTIN: Those hairs. Sprouting like pea shoots!

CHARLIE: Mum!

MRS BUCKTIN: How far up do they go?

She tries to check.

You and your father. Like bloody yaks.

She remains reading the paper, waiting for a retort. Nothing.

Back to CHARLIE …

Go and get dressed please.

CHARLIE: Mum—

MRS BUCKTIN: Go and put some clothes on. Now.

CHARLIE: There's … there's a wasp in my room.

MRS BUCKTIN: So?

CHARLIE: It's angry.

MRS BUCKTIN: Really? As angry as me?

CHARLIE: I'm … not sure.

MRS BUCKTIN: Go. And put. Some clothes on.

> CHARLIE *looks worried. He turns to us.*

CHARLIE: When my mother puts full stops between her words you know she's in a bad mood. But there's nothing that scares me more than insects. And I know that wasp is waiting for me in my room. Building its nest. Establishing an army. Wasps are mean buggers.

> *A beat.* CHARLIE *looks fearfully toward his bedroom.*

> MR BUCKTIN *leans across to a basket of laundry, fishes out a T-shirt and pants and hands them to his son, ruffling his hair.* CHARLIE *hurriedly puts on the clothes.* MR BUCKTIN *hides back behind the paper.*

MRS BUCKTIN: Charlie, if you're going to Jeffrey's today, I'd like you to stay on the street where I can see you, please.

CHARLIE: Why?

MRS BUCKTIN: Because I said so, that's why.

CHARLIE: How can that possibly be a reason?

MRS BUCKTIN: I'm your mother. I don't need a reason.

CHARLIE: That doesn't even make sense!

MRS BUCKTIN: Do. As you're bloody. Told.

> MRS BUCKTIN *glares at* CHARLIE.

> CHARLIE *turns to us again.*

CHARLIE: My mum's glare could make Errol Flynn flaccid.

> MR BUCKTIN *suddenly reappears from behind the newspaper.*

MR BUCKTIN: It's heating up in South-East Asia. Poor buggers. Maybe we should drive to the city and go to one of the marches.

MRS BUCKTIN: Drive all that way to take a bloody stroll with a bunch of bloody hippies? You've gotta be bloody joking.

> MR BUCKTIN *goes back to his paper.*

CHARLIE: But, Mum, you go to the city all the time.

MRS BUCKTIN: Excuse me, Lord Muck, I go to visit my family. I come from the city, not like the rest of you lot. When I go to the city, I'm going home. Don't you question my motives.

MR BUCKTIN *remains behind the newspaper.* CHARLIE *turns to us …*

CHARLIE: My dad, as ever, says nothing. [*To his parents*] I'm going to Jeffrey's.

MRS BUCKTIN: Remember. Stay. On. The. Street.

CHARLIE *grabs his satchel and walks out of the house.*

CHARLIE: [*to us*] The only thing I hate more than Mum's temper is Dad's silence. I know he's smart. I know he's got all kinds of things happening up there in his brain. But every time he comes close to letting it out, she shuts the door on it. Silence.

SCENE SEVEN

CHARLIE *is at the front of Jeffrey's house.*

CHARLIE: Oi, Jeffrey!

JEFFREY *peers out of his window.*

JEFFREY: None shall pass, Chuck.

CHARLIE: Huh?

JEFFREY: Grounded. You can't come in. I can't come out.

CHARLIE: What'd you do?

JEFFREY: Mum found out about swear words. Busted.

CHARLIE: What? But it's the summer holidays!

JEFFREY: I know. She won't even let me listen to the Test Match. I'm going *mental*. Do you know the score? Is Doug Walters in yet?

CHARLIE: I dunno.

JEFFREY: You're useless to me, Charlie. Useless.

A voice.

MRS LU: Hey! *Jeffrey, bạn và miệng bẩn thỉu của bạn không được rời khỏi nhà này, hiểu?* [Jeffrey, you and your filthy mouth are not leaving this house, understand?]

JEFFREY: Fuck. Gotta go.

He ducks back inside.

CHARLIE *turns. He sees* ELIZA *nearby. He freezes.*

She waves at him.

From left: Rachel Gordon as Mrs Bucktin, Ian Bliss as Mr Bucktin and Nicholas Denton as Charlie in Melbourne Theatre Company's 2016 production. (Photo: Jeff Busby)

Matilda Ridgway as Eliza and Tom Conroy as Charlie in Belvoir's 2016 production in Sydney. (Photo: Lisa Tomasetti)

He waves back.

She gestures for him to come to her.

CHARLIE *looks around to check she really means him.*

She smiles.

He takes a deep breath and walks toward her.

He tries to walk cool and calm, but ends up tripping over his own feet.

He composes himself.

ELIZA: You right?

CHARLIE: Yeah. Dangerous. Bloody council.

ELIZA: Well, I'll be sure to let my father know to put it on his agenda.

CHARLIE: Oh, I didn't mean—Sorry. I—

ELIZA: It's okay, Charlie. I'm joking.

> *Silence.* CHARLIE *doesn't know what to say.*

Well, I'd better get going. I just came out to read my book in the fresh air.

CHARLIE: What are you reading?

ELIZA: *Breakfast at Tiffany's*. Have you read it?

CHARLIE: Yeah … [*To us*] I haven't. I'll make sure I read it. Tonight.

ELIZA: I've seen the film four times but I haven't read the book. My mum says I'm not allowed to, but that's too bad. I've already started. I wish I lived in Manhattan like Holly Golightly.

CHARLIE: I'd like to live in Brooklyn, like the beat poets.

ELIZA: Well, I'll live in Manhattan and you can live in Brooklyn and we'll meet at the Plaza Hotel for high tea. I'll wear a fox-fur coat and penny loafers and you'll have a tartan scarf and a brown pinstripe suit. And a pipe.

CHARLIE: [*in a slightly lame American accent*] Sounds swell!

> ELIZA *smiles. Then …*

ELIZA: You wanna walk with me?

CHARLIE: [*to us*] I know Mum told me not to leave the street, but … something shifts in my pants and tells me to walk with Eliza. [*To* ELIZA] Sure.

They walk on a while.

ELIZA: Did you hear about Gertrude Baniszewski?

CHARLIE: Who's that?

ELIZA: A woman in America. She adopted two sisters named Jenny and
Sylvia Likens even though she already had seven children of her
own. The moment she got them inside her home she started doing
terrible things to Sylvia. She'd accuse her of stealing stuff just so she
could punish her. And she encouraged her other children to join in.
They'd stub cigarettes out on Sylvia's skin, they spat on her, stripped
her, beat her with a rod, lowered her into a bath of scalding water,
rubbed salt into her open wounds, knocked out her teeth, made her
eat her own vomit, piss and sh—

CHARLIE *stares wide-eyed at us.*

CHARLIE: [*to us*] The movement in my pants has well and truly stopped.

ELIZA *speaks matter-of-factly as they continue on.*

ELIZA: Then Gertrude Baniszewski decided to tattoo Sylvia. She and
her children burnt the word 'Whore' onto her stomach with a heated
needle. Sylvia fought back as much as she could. When they were
all out during the day she'd bang against the basement wall with
a shovel. But no-one came. Eventually, Sylvia died and was just
left in the hallway to rot. When the police came to investigate the
stench, they found her body. It wasn't until then that Jenny—Sylvia's
sister—gave them a note that said, 'If you take me with you, I'll tell
you everything'.

Silence.

CHARLIE: That's a really horrible story, Eliza.

ELIZA: I know.

CHARLIE: Why did you tell me that?

ELIZA: Why did she wait until then? The sister. Jenny. Why didn't she tell
someone at school? A neighbour? Anyone? She was Sylvia's only ally
and she didn't say a word. Why would she do that?

A beat. CHARLIE *is at a loss.*

I really better get home. I'm actually not supposed to be out.

CHARLIE: Are you grounded too?

ELIZA: Haven't you heard? It's all over the wireless.
CHARLIE: What is?
ELIZA: Laura went missing yesterday.

> CHARLIE *turns to us.*

CHARLIE: Corrigan has finally woken up.
ELIZA: My mother hasn't stopped crying and my dad, well …

> CHARLIE *remains silent.*

The police have been at my house all morning. I'm sick of it all. So I snuck out.
CHARLIE: Do they have any idea where she might be?
ELIZA: No. They haven't got a clue.

> *A beat.*

They're going to start searching soon. There's some special police coming from the city.
CHARLIE: There is? Oh, my stars.

> *A beat.*

ELIZA: I'd better go. My mum will be worried.
CHARLIE: You … you better hide the book from her if she doesn't want you to read it.

> ELIZA *calls over her shoulder.*

ELIZA: I'll tell her you gave it to me, Charlie.

> *She walks on.*

CHARLIE: Eliza …

> *She turns back to him.*

I hope they find your sister.
ELIZA: Me too.

> ELIZA *leaves.*

> CHARLIE *turns to us.*

CHARLIE: I know I should be worried about the city coppers, but right at this moment, I'm basking in the waft of air that Eliza has left behind. Every morning she must soak in a bath of lavender and rose petals and cinnamon and then spray herself with a silver atomiser filled with the finest perfume ever made. Probably by someone French with a massive nose and incredible olfactory skills.

SCENE EIGHT

CHARLIE *is slapped hard on the bum by* MRS BUCKTIN.

He stares at her stunned.

A beat.

She slaps him again, then calls inside.

MRS BUCKTIN: It's okay, Wesley! It's him!

>*She turns back to* CHARLIE.

Where the hell have you been?!

CHARLIE: At Jeffrey's!

>*She slaps him again.*

MRS BUCKTIN: That's bullshit, Charlie. I went there looking for you. Where have you been?

Tom Conroy as Charlie and Kate Mulvany as Mrs Bucktin in Belvoir's 2016 production in Sydney. (Photo: Lisa Tomasetti)

CHARLIE: Just a walk!

MRS BUCKTIN: I told you not to leave this street. It's dangerous out there. There's a bloody kidnapper in town and you're walking around like you own the place.

CHARLIE: What?

MRS BUCKTIN: Laura Wishart has gone missing. Do you understand now?

MRS BUCKTIN *hands* CHARLIE *a spade.*

Dig.

CHARLIE: Pardon?

MRS BUCKTIN: Start digging.

CHARLIE: What? Why?

MRS BUCKTIN: You'll find out later. When it's deep enough you can stop.

CHARLIE: Mum, it's boiling out here! I'll burn!

MRS BUCKTIN: Charlie, you will keep digging that hole till it's deep enough or you can spend the rest of this summer in your bedroom with the wasps and no books. Your choice.

CHARLIE *is seething. Caught.*

He takes the shovel.

He starts to dig.

MRS BUCKTIN *watches him for a moment then leaves.*

As he digs angrily, CHARLIE *talks to us.*

CHARLIE: As I keep digging, the hole turns into a kind of grave. The deeper I go, the more earthworms and caterpillars and centipedes I see. I think of Laura Wishart in the dam. Both of us stuck in our graves. Both of us holding onto secrets that the town is going to discover very, very soon.

He stabs at the ground furiously, digging and struggling.

MRS BUCKTIN *reappears.*

MRS BUCKTIN: Keep digging.

CHARLIE: Mum, I've got a blister.

MRS BUCKTIN: Only one? Keep digging.

CHARLIE: Mum!

MRS BUCKTIN: Charlie! Dig that bloody hole until you hit a Mexican, you hear me?

CHARLIE: No!

MRS BUCKTIN: And summer.

CHARLIE: No!

MRS BUCKTIN: And the rest of your teenage years. I will lock you away, boy.

CHARLIE: I wish you'd just piss off!

MRS BUCKTIN: Well, wish in one hand and shit in the other and see which one gets full first.

A beat. Another face-off.

Fill. It. In. I'm going to bridge.

CHARLIE *crumples.*

He climbs out of the pit and starts to fill in the hole.

MRS BUCKTIN *leaves.*

The lights begin to dim. The crickets start to chirp.

Finally ...

MR BUCKTIN *appears.*

MR BUCKTIN: Okay, Charlie. That's enough now.

CHARLIE *keeps filling the hole, in a furious trance.*

Charlie. Son ...

CHARLIE *stops. He collapses to his knees, exhausted.*

MR BUCKTIN *approaches him.*

Your mother's just worried, Charlie. Something very unsettling has happened and she just wants to keep you safe.

CHARLIE: Well, she's got a funny way of showing it.

MR BUCKTIN: It's not like you to disobey, Charlie. What's going on? Anything you want to tell me?

A beat.

CHARLIE *glances at us.*

He turns back to his father.

CHARLIE: No, Dad. She just makes me so bloody mad, that's all. Sorry for swearing.

MR BUCKTIN: You're a lot like her, you know.

CHARLIE: What? *Mum?! I. Am. Not!*

MR BUCKTIN: When it comes to dealing with your mother, Charlie, well, my advice is that concession doesn't necessarily mean defeat. Okay?

> CHARLIE *nods weakly.*

Good man. Now brush yourself off and come inside.

> MR BUCKTIN *goes to walk away.*

CHARLIE: Dad?

> MR BUCKTIN *turns.*

Where were you all day?

MR BUCKTIN: I was at the Miners' Hall. They're organising search parties for Laura Wishart.

CHARLIE: Do they know what's happened?

MR BUCKTIN: Early days yet, Charlie. Her parents have confirmed she was at home in bed on Thursday night and she wasn't there Friday morning. No signs of interference or a struggle. Do you know Laura well?

CHARLIE: Not really. I know her sister Eliza.

MR BUCKTIN: Well, I've taught Laura for a couple of years now. She's a very quiet, smart girl, but … very troubled too. Apparently she likes to go for walks at night but she always comes home. They're thinking she may have been meeting someone … somewhere. Have you ever heard anything about that, Charlie? At school, maybe?

CHARLIE: No.

> MR BUCKTIN *goes to leave again.* CHARLIE *calls out.*

Do the adults have any idea about it, Dad?

MR BUCKTIN: Everyone's got their opinion. People gossip like bloody spies in this town, Charlie. That's why your mum got a bit spooked when she couldn't find you. But don't worry. Laura will turn up. They always do.

> *A beat.*

I've made you a sandwich. It's inside. I'm going to my study.

CHARLIE: Can I come with you tomorrow to help with the search?

MR BUCKTIN: Absolutely not.

CHARLIE: But why not?

MR BUCKTIN: Because despite everything I just said … if we do find something, it might not be for the eyes of children.

He walks toward his study.

CHARLIE: [*to us*] I should tell him now. I know I should tell him now.

He turns to his father.

Dad …

A beat as MR BUCKTIN *waits.*

CHARLIE *can't say it.*

What do you do in there?

MR BUCKTIN: I read. Do a bit of marking. Read some more.

CHARLIE: That's all?

A beat.

MR BUCKTIN: That's all.

He wanders away. The light comes on in his study and he settles down, a silhouetted figure once more.

CHARLIE *watches the silhouette.*

CHARLIE: [*to us*] For the second time today, I can tell someone is not telling the truth. I know my dad is doing something else in that study. He leads a secret life that he doesn't want to share with the rest of us. And I guess I'm doing exactly the same, but mine is for the right reasons. Isn't it?

He sits down wearily on the sand pile.

MRS BUCKTIN *appears. She's giggly and drunk, and softly singing the chorus of Normie Rowe's 'Que Será Será'. She carries her shoes in her hand. She steps on the dirt.*

MRS BUCKTIN: *Fuck!*

She picks a doublegee from her foot.

Bloody doublegees.

All the while, CHARLIE *watches.*

MRS BUCKTIN *straightens herself. Lifts her head high.*

She walks, a little crookedly, into her home.

The lights fade to darkness.

CHARLIE: [*to us*] I need to see Jasper Jones. But … where is he?

As CHARLIE *settles down to sleep on the sand pile,* LAURA WISHART *wanders across the stage, past the sand pile, still wet and bloody.*

The mosquitoes continue their thrum.

SCENE NINE

Morning.

The thrumming of mozzies has become the drone of spotter planes.

Their dark shadows cross the stage.

CHARLIE *wakes with a start.*

CHARLIE: [*to us*] Spotter planes!

JEFFREY *hurries out into his own yard.*

JEFFREY: They must be searching for Laura Wishart, Charlie!

A beat.

Or her body. Arghghghghgh …

He wanders across to CHARLIE *like a zombie as the planes disappear.*

CHARLIE *turns to us* …

CHARLIE: Or are they looking for me? [*To* JEFFREY] I gotta get back inside.

As he heads in …

JEFFREY: Why are you covered in dirt?

CHARLIE: No reason.

JEFFREY: Have you been burying Laura's body?

CHARLIE *turns, stunned.*

CHARLIE: What? No! Why would you say that?

JEFFREY: Settle, petal. Just a joke.

CHARLIE: Well, it's not funny. I gotta stay inside.

He goes to walk away again. JEFFREY *stops him again.*

JEFFREY: Charlie … my family got killed yesterday.

CHARLIE *turns back to* JEFFREY.

CHARLIE: What?

JEFFREY: My aunt and uncle. Their village got bombed. In Vietnam.

CHARLIE: Jeffrey …

JEFFREY *nods.*

JEFFREY: Mum and Dad are pretty sad. Mum thinks those spotter planes are bombers coming to get her now too. She's hiding under the bed.

CHARLIE: Did your aunt and uncle have children?

JEFFREY: A boy and a girl. They're really little. They're okay. My dad has been on the phone all night trying to get them to come here and stay with us but it's hard to do that sort of thing.

CHARLIE: But they're orphans now. They should be with their family.

JEFFREY *shrugs.*

JEFFREY: We're trying, but … maybe the further away you are, the less you have to care.

Silence.

Last night Mum was so angry she even started yelling *'Fuck'. Fuck* this and *fuck* that. It was pretty weird.

CHARLIE: Wow.

JEFFREY: You should've seen my dad. He was so shocked. He looked at me like it was my fault.

CHARLIE: The bomb?

JEFFREY: No, the swearing.

A beat.

Charlie … if you had the choice, would you rather not know when you were going to die and have it surprise you, or know your whole life the exact time and dread it coming?

CHARLIE: I haven't given it much thought.

JEFFREY: I'd wanna know. So I could cram as much in as possible.

A beat.

Do you believe in heaven? The place where you get to sit on a cloud and take harp lessons and play volleyball in the nude?

A beat.

CHARLIE: I haven't given it much thought.

JEFFREY: Well, whatever people believe, I'd rather do all that stuff right now than wait till I'm dead. I guess my aunt and uncle didn't get that chance. I sure hope they like volleyball.

He gives a sad grin and trudges back to his house.

As he does, the spotter planes fly over him once more.

JEFFREY *stares up at them before departing.*

CHARLIE *enters his sleep-out and speaks to us ...*

CHARLIE: For someone who has never given death much thought, I've certainly made up for it this week. I've thought of nothing else. I even forgot about Christmas till Mum shoved a plate of cold turkey into my room.

Faint Christmas carols play.

I just wait. I wait. I wait to see what happens next.

The lights fade.

JASPER *is hauled onto the stage by dark* MEN *in uniform.*

Harry Tseng (left) as Jeffrey and Nicholas Denton as Charlie in Melbourne Theatre Company's 2016 production. (Photo: Jeff Busby)

As Laura Wishart decomposes in her watery grave and the spotter planes fly overhead and the city coppers arrive in their glossy cars, and worried parents hurry their children inside to unwrap their presents, and Mad Jack Lionel washes the blood from his hands, I wait.

JASPER *is beaten and kicked.*

I wait.

JASPER *is kicked and beaten.*

The sound of MAD JACK *calling 'Jasper' is heard faintly, over and over ...*

I wait.

The MEN *leave* JASPER *in a broken mess.*

The eerie calling stops.

CHARLIE *waits in his room, peering through the louvres.*

And still, Jasper Jones doesn't come.

END OF ACT ONE

ACT TWO

SCENE ONE

The exact same image that started Act One.

The only sound is the cricking of summer cicadas.

From the louvred window of a sleep-out comes the glow of a kerosene lamp. Inside the room is CHARLIE BUCKTIN. *Only this time, he isn't reading a book.*

He's waiting.

Then ...

A dark creeping figure makes its way deftly, silently toward the sleep-out. CHARLIE *does not see the figure.*

A beat.

The figure looks around nervously, then raps lightly on the window. CHARLIE *turns, startled. Then looks to us.*

CHARLIE: Jasper Jones has come to my window.

> *He hurriedly removes the slats and keeps talking as he climbs out.*

Where have you been, Jasper? It's been a whole week! I thought you were gone for good! I've been hiding inside for days pretending I've got the runs. Actually, I have got the runs. Might've been Mum's turkey. My gut's all twisted and jumpy. And every time one of those spotter planes flies over or a copper drives down the street I just need to poo. I can't help it, but I—

> *He sees* JASPER*'s face in the moonlight. It is beaten badly.*

What happened to your face?!

JASPER: Tell you later. Come on. We gotta go.

> *He starts to walk away hurriedly.* CHARLIE *follows.*

CHARLIE: Where have you been?

JASPER: Around.

CHARLIE: Did you have a merry Christmas?

JASPER: Was it Christmas? Didn't notice.

CHARLIE: They've been having patrols through Corrigan, Jasper. Every night. I don't reckon it's safe for us to be out like this.

JASPER: Most of the town is at the Sovereign, getting pissed. No patrols tonight, Charlie.

They walk on.

CHARLIE *turns to us.*

CHARLIE: Everything and nothing happened in the past week. Kids were heading back onto the street, trying out their new Christmas toys, but only till dusk. Parents were locking doors and looking at each other with suspicion. The Ashes were a draw—not even Dougie Walters could save it. Mum was still angry. Dad was still invisible. The city search crews had come and gone. Only locals could stand being in this town for longer than a few days. The latest round of draft letters were delivered and a few of the local teens were packing their bags to head off to Vietnam.

JASPER: Keep up, Charlie.

CHARLIE: [*to us*] At a meeting at the Miners' Hall last night, Mrs Findlay, the publican's wife, screamed at Jeffrey's mum. Told her to go back to where she came from. Then she pulled out a big chunk of Mrs Lu's hair. Apparently one of Mrs Findlay's sons got drafted. Everyone rushed to her after it happened … but no-one helped Mrs Lu.

They arrive at Mad Jack's place.

The peaches hang from the tree.

JASPER *glares at the house.*

JASPER: I'll get you, you bastard.

They walk on.

CHARLIE: Are you still sure it was him, Jasper?

JASPER: Think about it, Charlie. For years he's bin comin' out that door and callin' my name, whenever I've walked past. 'Jasper! Jasper!' And he's seen Laura too. Seen me with her. But starting from that night one week ago, I haven't seen him once.

CHARLIE: That doesn't make him a murderer. Does it?

They are back at the grove.

SCENE TWO

A long moment.

The boys take in their surrounds.

Then ...

JASPER: Someone else has bin here.
CHARLIE: Who? The killer? The cops? Who?
JASPER: I dunno. But someone.

> *A beat.*

> CHARLIE *looks around, terrified. Then ...*

CHARLIE: Got any whiskey?

> JASPER *looks surprised, then gets out a bottle.*

JASPER: Here you go. Fill yer boots.

> *He looks down at* CHARLIE*'s feet.*

Well ... yer sandals.

> CHARLIE *takes a swig as he takes in* JASPER*'s face.*

CHARLIE: Your dad do that to you?
JASPER: Nah. Dad skipped town last Friday. Haven't seen him.
CHARLIE: Last Friday? He left the day after Laura died?
JASPER: It wasn't him. He's a mean old bastard, but he's no murderer.
CHARLIE: So who did that to your face?
JASPER: Come on, mate. The coppers.
CHARLIE: The police? City or local?
JASPER: All of 'em. They asked me in for a visit and locked me up the
   entire weekend.
CHARLIE: Can they do that?
JASPER: They can do anything they like with their shiny badges and
   steel-capped boots.
CHARLIE: But why? Why would they do that to you?
JASPER: Cos they reckon I got somethin' to do with Laura bein' missin'.
   They wanted me to confess to somethin'.
CHARLIE: What did you tell them?
JASPER: Nuthin'. And that's why I couldn't breathe right till yesterday.

I told 'em nuthin'. And what I learned was that they know nuthin'. They haven't got a clue where she is. We're still in the clear, Charlie.

CHARLIE: There's some people who reckon she ran away.

JASPER: She'd never leave Corrigan without me. We made a promise to each other. Besides, we know where she is, Charlie.

CHARLIE: But no-one else does. They reckon she's hitchhiking to the city. Laura's dad was on the news, asking people to keep their eyes out.

JASPER lifts his shirt.

JASPER: See that bootprint? That's from Mr Wishart.

He points to his face.

And that one? That's his right hook.

A mark on his neck.

And this one? That's where he burned me with his cigarette.

CHARLIE: What?

JASPER: Wasn't just the coppers that laid into me, Charlie. Laura's old man was there too. Screaming at me, *'What have you done to my little girl?'*

He mimes punching and kicking.

Bam! Bam! Bam! *'Where is she?'* Bam! Bam! Bam! *'I'll kill you, you little coon!'* Bam!

CHARLIE: But he's the shire president.

JASPER: You don't believe me?

CHARLIE: It's not that, it's just …

A beat.

He points to a large scar on JASPER*'s arm.*

What about that one, Jasper? Who did that to you?

JASPER: I've always had that one.

They drift into silence and drink on.

Look at that moon, Charlie. You reckon someone will get there someday?

CHARLIE: We can't even get to the bottom of the ocean, let alone all the way up there.

JASPER: We're just specks, Charlie. Specks of specks of specks. It's all bigger than us, so there's no point in trying to be bigger than we are.

And no bearded bloke in the sky is gonna give us a lift up just cos
we chuck money in a tray and eat fish on Fridays.
CHARLIE: Sometimes I think believing in God is a bit like closing a door
when there's a cold draught. It's still cold out there, it's just that you
don't notice it cos you're nice and warm.

> *A beat.*

What you just said—is that what Aboriginals believe in, Jasper?
JASPER: I dunno. My mum was Aboriginal, but I never really knew her.
CHARLIE: What happened to her?
JASPER: Car accident when I was a baby. That's all my old man ever
told me.

> *Suddenly,* LAURA *appears from the dam. She points at* CHARLIE.
> CHARLIE *stares at her wide-eyed as she stands before him,
> dripping, but* JASPER *doesn't notice her.*

CHARLIE: Oh, my God. Jasper …

> *He points back at* LAURA.

JASPER: What is it, mate?
CHARLIE: Jasper …

> CHARLIE *keels over.* LAURA *keeps her arm raised, pointing.*

JASPER: You drunk again, Charlie?

> CHARLIE *starts to dry retch. He crawls around the stage, all the
> while watching* LAURA *as she stares at him, her pointed arm never
> moving.*

Hold on, mate. Here … drink this.

> JASPER *fills a cup from the dam and gives it to* CHARLIE.

> CHARLIE *takes it and skulls it down.*

> LAURA *remains standing, pointing.*

> CHARLIE *speaks to us drunkenly.*

CHARLIE: I am filled with dam water. With the flecks and flakes of Laura
Wishart's pale skin. Bits of her body. Her long blonde hair. The specks
and specks and specks of her.

> CHARLIE *stares around wide-eyed, sobering up a little.*

He sits up and stares at what LAURA *was pointing at. The tree trunk.*

He goes to the trunk and pulls away some leaves at its base, as LAURA *leaves.*

Jasper …

JASPER *turns.*

Look.

Scrawled on the trunk is the word 'Sorry'.

The two boys look at one another, stunned.

JASPER & CHARLIE: [*together*] 'Sorry'.

SCENE THREE

CHARLIE *and* JASPER *hurry back through town.*

CHARLIE: [*to us*] Jasper was right. Someone *had* been to his spot. Maybe even tonight. Not only that, but they'd confessed. They'd written 'Sorry' right there on the tree trunk, right under where they'd hanged Laura Wishart. Maybe they'd gone back expecting her to still be there, swinging from that eucalypt.

A spotlight is suddenly cast across CHARLIE *and* JASPER.

JASPER: Charlie! Get down!

The two boys squat in the shadows.

The patrol cars are back. Somethin' must've happened.

They sneak on and a light flashes over them again.

CHARLIE: Who do you think they're after, Jasper? Is it us? Oh, my God, is it us?

JASPER *leads* CHARLIE *on. They are nearly caught again by the spotlight as they reach Charlie's street.*

Flashing police lights.

JASPER: Fuck.

He pulls CHARLIE *to him.*

Charlie, don't say nuthin'. *Nuthin'*. Unnerstand?

CHARLIE: But what do I do?!

JASPER: Just walk over there and make somethin' up. Just don't say nuthin' about me or it's all over. They don't suspect you, Charlie. You haven't done nuthin' wrong.

CHARLIE *starts to breathe heavily, panicking. He doesn't move.*

Charlie, look at me. See them coppers in your front yard? They're the bastards that hit me and kicked me and burnt me. They see me here with you, they're gonna do much worse. I have to go, mate. But don't worry—I'll come back.

CHARLIE: Please don't leave me, Jasper.

JASPER: You're just gonna have to get brave in a hurry now, Charlie. Unnerstand?

CHARLIE *slowly walks toward his house and the police.*

JASPER *disappears into the shadows as silhouetted townsfolk appear and watch* CHARLIE *approach the scene.*

CHARLIE: I am a dead man walking.

Suddenly, CHARLIE *is fully lit by a spotlight.*

A wail from MRS BUCKTIN *as she grabs* CHARLIE *and holds him.*

MRS BUCKTIN: Charlie! Where have you been? We were so afraid! We were so *afraid*!

A POLICE OFFICER *appears beside her.*

OFFICER: You've caused quite a ruckus tonight, my boy.

MRS BUCKTIN: You snuck out of your room! Disappeared without a trace!

OFFICER: Quite the ruckus.

MRS BUCKTIN: Charlie … have you been? With Jasper. Jones?

An inhalation of breath from the OFFICER.

CHARLIE: I … I … I'm in love with Eliza Wishart.

MRS BUCKTIN: What?

CHARLIE: I haven't been able to sleep, you see. I keep thinking of her lying awake, waiting for her sister to come home. I just wanted to comfort her, see—Eliza—cos I realised she must be really, really sad about everything. So I snuck out to see her tonight, to check she was okay.

OFFICER: Awwww. Sweet.

CHARLIE: That night you made me dig the hole, Mum, I'd tried to do the same thing. I was too embarrassed to tell you.

OFFICER: What hole?

MRS BUCKTIN: Nothing important. Nothing. Keep going, darling.

CHARLIE: When I saw the patrol cars out tonight I got scared and hid. I thought maybe they were hunting down a baddie. So I laid low in a front yard down the road there. I'm sorry. I didn't mean to cause any trouble for you and Dad.

OFFICER: Where is your husband now?

MRS BUCKTIN: He's gone looking. But normally he's in the nursery.

CHARLIE: The study.

The OFFICER *leans in close to* CHARLIE.

OFFICER: I admire your intent, little man. Love's a wonderful commodity. But remember Romeo and Juliet. If either of them had exercised some common sense things mightn't have turned out so shit. Think on that.

He tips his hat to MRS BUCKTIN.

Ruthy.

The OFFICER *walks away.*

MRS BUCKTIN *and* CHARLIE *stare at each other for a long moment.*

MRS BUCKTIN: You. Are grounded. Until nineteen. Sixty. Six.

She storms away.

CHARLIE: That's next week!

MRS BUCKTIN: Nineteen seventy-one!

She's gone.

SCENE FOUR

CHARLIE *speaks to us as he climbs into his sleep-out.*

CHARLIE: And so I am banished to my sleep-out. At first I try to lose myself in my books. I have a new Truman Capote novel about a terrible murder in a small town, but every time I try to read it, it feels like insects crawling over my scalp and down my spine. So mostly, I spend my time writing. Obsessively. Not my Great Australian Novel though. Mostly poems about trees. And flowers.

And Eliza. Sometimes all three at once. Until my poems turn into daydreams set in a Manhattan ballroom where, for once, with Eliza, I have all the right words …

> ELIZA *appears onstage in a ball gown.* CHARLIE *takes her in his arms. They begin to dance …* ELIZA *speaks in an American accent.*

ELIZA: Look, Charlie! Over there with Capote! It's Harper Lee!

CHARLIE: And there by the bar—Ernest Hemingway!

ELIZA: Over in the corner—see?—poor little Sylvia Plath …

CHARLIE: And up on the balcony—Roald Dahl!

ELIZA: Oh, I don't read Dahl. I'm not interested in chocolate factories, Charlie. What have they got to do with real life?

CHARLIE: Quite, my darling Eliza. Quite … Another martini?

ELIZA: Well, golly gee damn yes!

> *They dance on …* ELIZA *is suddenly very serious.*

Promise me one thing, Charlie—don't take me home till I'm drunk. Very drunk indeed …

> *They dance on.* ELIZA *swirls offstage, leaving* CHARLIE *alone once more, still lost in his reverie.*

> WARWICK *and* CLARRY *appear.*

WARWICK: Oi! Fuck! Get out of my way, you fucken four-eyed fruit!

> CLARRY *chuckles.*

SCENE FIVE

A cricket match forms.

CHARLIE: Finally, Mum gets sick of me at home and I'm released from house arrest. The first thing I do is go find Jeffrey.

> JEFFREY *is fielding. He sees* CHARLIE *and waves.*

JEFFREY: Hey, Charlie! Guess who's got two thumbs and is *officially* playing in this game?!

CHARLIE: Huh?

JEFFREY: This guy!

CHARLIE: What? But how?

JEFFREY: Jim Quincy's appendix exploded. They reckon it was his mum's Christmas cake. So I'm in!

CHARLIE: They're letting you play?

JEFFREY: They're pretty pissed off, but I was the only option. I mean really, they should've made me captain. This field is an outrage. You need a third slip for this batter. He's like a spider monkey. He won't stop swinging. Couldn't hit a cow's arse with a banjo.

WARWICK: Oi! Cong! Focus on the game, you little slapfaced bastard.

JEFFREY: No worries, Warwick!

He waves.

CHARLIE: How's your mum going, Jeffrey?

JEFFREY: She's alright. She's wearing her hair out so no-one can see the bald patch.

CHARLIE: Ouch.

JEFFREY: Dad's gone kinda weird though. A bunch of blokes got laid off from the mine, but he didn't. He's been getting a hard time from the guys that are left. They're treating him like some kind of Bond villain. Hey, would you rather wear a hat made of spiders or have penises for fingers?

CHARLIE: Are the spiders alive?

JEFFREY: Yes.

CHARLIE: Are they poisonous?

JEFFREY: Yes.

CHARLIE: Then penis fingers. Definitely.

A whistle.

WARWICK: Oi! Changeover, cunts!

JEFFREY: Gotta go! Time for a bat! What do you reckon, Charlie? Reckon they'll put me in the top order?

CHARLIE: Not a chance.

As JEFFREY *runs away …*

JEFFREY: Sassytime, Chuck! Whoooooooooo!

JEFFREY points to ELIZA *who has appeared behind him.*

ELIZA: Hello, Charlie.

CHARLIE: Hell … hello.

ELIZA sits down beside him. CHARLIE *inhales surreptitiously.*

ELIZA: When is Jeffrey batting?

CHARLIE: From the looks of things, probably sometime tonight when the teams have gone home.

> *They sit in silence.* ELIZA *suddenly reaches out and touches* CHARLIE*'s shirt.*

ELIZA: I like your shirt.
CHARLIE: Thank you. I like your smell.
ELIZA: Thank you.

> *A beat.*

CHARLIE: How is your family?
ELIZA: Christmas was really weird. Mum had already bought presents for Laura so she wrapped them all up and gave them to me. Then she said I'll have to give them back to Laura when she comes home. And Dad … well, Dad is acting like he never really had a daughter.

> ELIZA *starts to cry a little.* CHARLIE *gives her a handkerchief from his pocket.*

CHARLIE: It's okay. There's no snot.

> ELIZA *dabs her face.*

ELIZA: You know those days when you get the Mean Reds?
CHARLIE: The Mean Reds?
ELIZA: Not the blues. The blues are when you just feel a bit sad. The Mean Reds are different. The Mean Reds are when you don't know what you're afraid of.

> *A beat.*

I'm not a good person, Charlie. I don't even know why you talk to me.

> *A beat.*

> CHARLIE *clears his throat. He gets a piece of paper from his pocket and reads it.*

CHARLIE: A tree.
A tree
Doesn't know it's a tree.
It doesn't know how pretty its flowers are
Or how beautiful they smell
Or how soft and sweet its fruit is.

It can't feel how warm I am with my arms around it.

It can't hear me when I tell it these things.

It doesn't know anything.

I'm glad you're not a tree.

A beat.

That's a poem I wrote. Hey. Would you rather have a hat made of spiders or penises for fingers?

ELIZA: Are the spiders alive?

CHARLIE: I'm afraid so.

ELIZA: And are they poisonous?

CHARLIE: Absolutely. Oozing—

ELIZA: Then penis fingers.

CHARLIE: Me too!

ELIZA: Good. Then we can go live in New York in the winter. And we'll wear mittens to hide our hideous penis fingers.

A beat.

Charlie, look! Jeffrey's batting!

CHARLIE *speaks to us.*

CHARLIE: It's true! Corrigan's wickets have fallen one after the other and I hadn't even noticed. Now, Jeffrey Lu, the last man in, is marching to the crease.

JEFFREY *appears with a bat. He waves to the crowd and takes his place at the crease.*

JEFFREY: Check it out, Charlie! Just like Dougie Walters!

JEFFREY *starts to bat.*

CHARLIE: The Corrigan side are acting like the game is already lost. The coach is already packing up the gear. No-one is paying Jeffrey the slightest bit of attention except me and Eliza and the bowler ... And then ...

JEFFREY *whacks a ball.*

Jeffrey starts to bat. Like ... *really* bat. He shows no signs of panic or pressure. He's playing smart and sure, tussling with the spinner.

JEFFREY *plays on.*

ELIZA: He's really good!

CHARLIE: The next bowler steps up and Jeffrey drives on—hitting twos and threes, picking the gaps with amazing precision. He has seriously taken this game by the nuts.

CHARLIE *calls out.*

Go, Jeffrey!

JEFFREY *bats on.*

The remaining crowd are suddenly drawn to the sidelines. Even Warwick has stopped packing his things and has started pacing the ground.

ELIZA: Must be close.

CHARLIE: There's only six balls left.

ELIZA *takes* CHARLIE*'s hand excitedly. His jaw drops in amazement.*

JEFFREY *bats on.*

CHARLIE *speaks like a commentator.*

Jeffrey bats and runs but the bowler shoves him as he passes. The crowd is furious. Finally the crowd are on the little man's side!

JEFFREY *bats again.*

The next ball Jeffrey punches through the cover—zipping in two runs. The crowd starts yelling, 'Shot, Cong!', and suddenly that terrible insult has become a kind of nickname.

JEFFREY *bats on.*

Next ball and Jeffrey places brilliantly down fine leg and he grabs another two runs.

The crowd are cheering, 'Cong! Cong! Cong! Cong!'

JEFFREY *bats on.*

Fourth ball and Jeffrey swings. Caught by the wickie but there's been no connection. The crowd sigh with relief.

ELIZA: I can hardly watch …

She rests her head on CHARLIE*'s shoulder.*

CHARLIE: The next ball is a high bouncer. The crowd protests …

WARWICK: Wide! *Wide,* ump!

CHARLIE: But to no avail.

> JEFFREY *looks exhausted. He wipes the sweat from his brow and squints at the bowler.*

There's one ball left. I'm not sure how many runs we need, but by the looks of things, there's a good chance we could win this if Jeffrey gets willow on leather. The crowd … the crowd are really hollering! They really want Jeffrey to do this!

> *To himself …*

Come on, Jeffrey.

> JEFFREY *lines up at the crease.*
>
> *In slow motion, the bowler delivers the ball.*
>
> JEFFREY *adjusts as the ball is in flight. Then … he knocks the ball masterfully.*
>
> *Corrigan erupts.*

He's done it! He's bloody done it!

ELIZA: Whoo, Jeffrey! Whooooo!

> JEFFREY *raises his arms as the sounds of a celebration become a roar.*
>
> ELIZA *and* CHARLIE *embrace excitedly. And then …*
>
> *The sounds of the cricket celebration drown away as* ELIZA *and* CHARLIE *kiss.*
>
> *Long, lingering and gentle. Staring into one another's eyes.*
>
> *Suddenly …*

JEFFREY: Sassytime!

> ELIZA *and* CHARLIE *part hurriedly, embarrassed.*

Did you guys see what I just did out there or were you too busy tasting each other's tonsils?

ELIZA: We saw. You were amazing!

JEFFREY: Forty-three runs! Jeffrey Lu on debut! I'm the town hero! Come on, Charlie. We gotta go. I wanna tell my parents what happened before it gets published in the *Wisden.*

CHARLIE: Go on without me.

JEFFREY: Charlie, I'm buggered. You gotta help me carry my stuff home. It's an honour, you know.

CHARLIE *turns to* ELIZA.

CHARLIE: Um … I gotta go.
ELIZA: I know.
CHARLIE: You wanna walk with us?
ELIZA: No. I'm gonna stay here and read my book. With my penis fingers.
CHARLIE: Okay.
ELIZA: Okay.
CHARLIE: Okay.
ELIZA: Okay.

An awkward silence as they look to JEFFREY *who is watching them, amused. He rolls his eyes.*
JEFFREY: Okay …

He turns his back to them.

CHARLIE *leans in to kiss* ELIZA *but it's all pretty awkward now.*
CHARLIE: Oop. Sorry.
ELIZA: It's fine.
CHARLIE: I kissed your eye.
ELIZA: It's okay. Bye, Charlie.
CHARLIE: Bye, Eliza.

JEFFREY *mocks them.*

JEFFREY: 'Bye, Charlie … Bye, Eliza … Sasssssssytime … '

As they travel, CHARLIE *turns to us …*

CHARLIE: I know Jeffrey feels like Superman today, but not as much as me. I'm the Man of Steel and I've got Lois Lane by my side and I'm avenging all the wrongs in this town.

JEFFREY *hurries away with his gear.*

JEFFREY: Bye, Charlie. Forty-three! Jeffrey Lu on debut! Whoooooo!

He's gone. CHARLIE *continues onto his own house.*

CHARLIE: But deep down I'm scared. Now I've kissed Eliza, I feel even worse about Laura. I know I should tell Eliza there is no 'when' Laura is coming back. Laura Wishart is not coming back. Because after she died I drowned her to save Jasper Jones. I did that. I hope Jasper Jones comes round tonight. I wanna ask him if he discovered anything more while I was under house arrest. I wanna tell him I did the right thing by him and didn't dob. But most of all, I wanna tell him I kissed Eliza Wishart. And that, miracle of miracles, she kissed me right back.

SCENE SIX

Darkness.

The peaches glow on the peach tree at Mad Jack Lionel's place.

JASPER *appears and snoops across the property. He peers around warily, looking for clues.*

Then ... LAURA WISHART *appears.*

She stands before JASPER *and once again raises a pointed finger.*

JASPER *doesn't see her but it's clear he feels a presence. He follows the direction of the point. He looks to a shadowed area of the stage. There is a wreck of a car. Illuminated on the car is the word 'Sorry'.*

JASPER *backs away.*

Suddenly ... a large looming figure appears in the doorway. MAD JACK LIONEL. JASPER *stares at him. Raises his finger and points.*

JASPER: I knew it was you! *I knew it was you! Fuckin' murderer!*

> *He turns and runs ...*

> *And suddenly he is with* CHARLIE.

SCENE SEVEN

CHARLIE: It might just be a coincidence.

JASPER: Think about it. Jack Lionel has always had it in for me. We know he's murdered before. And now he's scratching his guilt all over the place. That word 'Sorry'—it's on the car at his place and it's on the tree at my place.

CHARLIE: But why haven't the police been to see him then?

JASPER: The police in this town are idiots, Charlie. They still don't even know Laura's dead.

CHARLIE: Well, what do we do now?

> *A beat.*

JASPER: Now we gotta get him to confess.

CHARLIE: How do we do that?!

JASPER: Tomorrow night. The whole town will be at the Miners' Hall to watch the fireworks. But not us. We're going to Mad Jack Lionel's.

CHARLIE: Jasper, I've never even stolen a *peach* from Mad Jack, let alone accused him of cold-blooded murder!

JASPER: You don't have to say anythin', Charlie. Just leave the talkin' to me. You just gotta be there as a witness.

CHARLIE: Witness to what?

JASPER: I'm gonna tell him we saw him kill Laura and that if he doesn't turn himself in, we'll do it for him.

CHARLIE: But we didn't see him kill her.

JASPER: It's just a tactic, Charlie. Back him into a corner.

> *A beat.*

Look, if it's just my word against his, I ain't got a chance with the coppers, but if you're there as a witness, they'll believe us fersure.

> CHARLIE *still looks dubious.*

Don't you think we owe it to the Wisharts, Charlie? Don't you think it's about time they knew the truth about what happened to Laura?

CHARLIE: I guess so.

JASPER: Okay. I'll see you tomorrow night.

> *A figure appears ...*

Who's that?

CHARLIE: Mum. She's been at bridge.

> MRS BUCKTIN *walks drunkenly along the stage, her dress unbuttoned.*
>
> *She doesn't notice the boys watching her. She straightens her hair, then wanders on toward the house ...*

MRS BUCKTIN: *I'm home!*

> *Silence. She walks inside, demoralised.*

JASPER: Bridge, huh?

CHARLIE: Yeah.

JASPER: She play bridge a lot, your mum?

CHARLIE: Yeah.

A beat.

JASPER: Remember, Charlie … tomorrow night. I'll meet you at Mad
Jack's.

CHARLIE: You're not gonna walk there with me?

JASPER: We can't be seen together, Charlie. You gotta get brave, mate.
See you tomorrow.

And he is gone.

CHARLIE: Sorry.

A beat.

Sorry. [*To us*] In all the best books I've read, the characters are caught
between being good and being bad. They're stuck between right and
wrong. But it's the truly good people that can tell the difference. And
so it's a truly good person that can admit fault and say, 'Sorry'. Eric
Edgar Cooke never whispered it. Gertrude Baniszewski never burned
it into Sylvia Likens' skin, I'm sure. Sorry belongs to the truly good
people. It means you feel the pulse of someone else's pain and it's
an offering for someone who's suffering to take or leave. Sorry. Or
is sorry the refuge of the weak? Because tomorrow, the last day of
nineteen sixty-five, I have a feeling I'm gonna be sorry. Real sorry.
'Cause I don't know if I'm gonna make it to nineteen sixty-six.

He settles into bed.

Darkness.

*An angry mob tears up the Lus' flowerbed, screaming, 'Red rat!
Red rat!'*

LAURA WISHART *appears.*

*She stands amid the debris for a long moment, watching the shad-
owy mob.*

She leaves. The mob departs.

Silence. The garden is ruined.

SCENE EIGHT

The lights rise.

A new day. 31 December 1965.

JEFFREY *sits amid the floral detritus and eats watermelon. He spits seeds. There is something different about his demeanour. His spark has diminished and he looks haunted.*

CHARLIE *appears and takes in the spectacle.*

CHARLIE: Oh, my God, Jeffrey. What happened last night?
JEFFREY: Some blokes turned up in a ute. They ripped up Dad's flowers and then bashed him.

> *He spits a seed.*

CHARLIE: Why?
JEFFREY: Because they got laid off from the mine and he didn't. They were calling him a red rat. They were pretty drunk.

> *He spits another seed.*

CHARLIE: What did your dad do?
JEFFREY: Nothing he could do. They beat the shit out of him. Four onto one. I tried my Bruce Lee one-inch punch, but I … reckon I'm yet to master it fully.

> *He spits another seed. He doesn't even look at* CHARLIE.

Say thanks to your dad for us.
CHARLIE: Why?
JEFFREY: He came out of nowhere. Like he was Superman. Just walked across the lawn and broke up the fight. Just tore those blokes off my dad like they weighed nothin' at all. One after the other.
CHARLIE: Wait … *my* dad did that?
JEFFREY: I reckon if he hadn't showed up, those bastards might have …

> *He spits a seed.*

Anyway.
CHARLIE: They tore up his garden.
JEFFREY: Yep.
CHARLIE: All gone.

> *They stare at the flowers.*

> JEFFREY *passes* CHARLIE *some watermelon.*

JEFFREY: Here. Spit. I wanna start a new garden for Dad. And nothing grows faster than a watermelon patch.

CHARLIE: It's not quite the same.
JEFFREY: It's a start.

> *They spit.*

CHARLIE: Hey, Jeffrey … I'm not coming to the fireworks tonight.
JEFFREY: What? But it's New Year's Eve!
CHARLIE: I know. I'm sorry. I just … Mum's still not letting me out at night.
JEFFREY: But won't Eliza be there? Don't you wanna sneak out for some sassytime under the sparklers?
CHARLIE: Shut up.
JEFFREY: Don't you wanna see her so you can hold hands and serenade her with panpipes and share food mouth-to-mouth like birds?
CHARLIE: Panpipes?
JEFFREY: It's in their fizzyology, my friend. Girls cannot resist bamboo flutes. Fact.

> CHARLIE *stands.*

CHARLIE: I gotta go.
JEFFREY: But it's not even dark yet.
CHARLIE: It's just … I gotta do stuff. At home.
JEFFREY: What, read a romance? Write a love poem? Rub a picture of Eliza all over your naked body like soap?
CHARLIE: Nah, just … stuff.

> *He stands awkwardly, then suddenly embraces* JEFFREY.

JEFFREY: Queer!
CHARLIE: Nah, I'm just … sorry about your dad's flowers.
JEFFREY: They were Queen Elizabeth's anyway.

> *A beat.*

Well … I gotta practise my punch and work out where I'm going wrong.

> *He spits a watermelon seed.*

CHARLIE: See you next year, idiot.

> CHARLIE *walks away.*
>
> ELIZA *appears suddenly.*

ELIZA: There you are! I've been looking everywhere for you.
CHARLIE: Wha … what are you doing out?
ELIZA: What do you mean? The whole town's out. Fireworks. Come on.

> *She drags him by the hand.*

CHARLIE: I'm not going.
ELIZA: Why not?
CHARLIE: It's just … I'm going to something else. I can't say where. I just …
ELIZA: Charlie. It's important I see you tonight. I need to tell you something. Please.
CHARLIE: I'll come back later.
ELIZA: Do you promise? Cross your heart?
CHARLIE: Cross my heart.
ELIZA: And hope to die?

> CHARLIE *nods.* ELIZA *leans in to kiss him but he backs away.*

CHARLIE: Goodbye, Eliza.

> *He stumbles away.*

> *Darkness falls.*

[*To us*] Tonight we confront the town killer. Mad Jack Lionel. And I can't help but think, 'Is this my final night too?' This man has no qualms about murdering women, so he'll have no problem killing me and Jasper. And there's no-one in the whole town that knows what we know. If we die tonight, how will Laura be avenged? And who will know where to find her body, as well as ours?

SCENE NINE

CHARLIE *arrives at Mad Jack's. The peaches glow on the tree.*

JASPER *is nowhere to be seen.*

CHARLIE *waits in the darkness, looking around edgily.*

JASPER *makes his way through the shadows toward* CHARLIE.

JASPER: Charlie.

> CHARLIE *screams.*

Shhhhh … Come on. Let's go.

He starts to walk toward a door.

CHARLIE: Now?

JASPER: You gotta get brave, Charlie. Come on.

They make their way slowly toward the house. Closer ... Then ...

MAD JACK *appears.*

CHARLIE *and* JASPER *stop, startled.*

MAD JACK: Jasper! Good God, is that you?

JASPER *glares at* MAD JACK.

Strike a light, what a surprise! Come in! Come in, the both of you.

He reaches for JASPER.

JASPER: We're not comin' in. We're here to talk about what happened.

MAD JACK: I see.

JASPER: We know it was you. We know you did it.

MAD JACK: I've been waiting for this.

JASPER: So you admit it. You admit that you killed her?

MAD JACK *nods.*

Hayden Spencer (left) as Mad Jack and Guy Simon as Jasper in Melbourne Theatre Company's 2016 production. (Photo: Jeff Busby)

MAD JACK: Jasper, I know you're upset. I always thought you'd have worked it out sooner, though. Who told you? Your dad?

JASPER: Nobody told me nuthin'.

MAD JACK: Well, then how did you find out?

JASPER: We *saw* you. Me and Charlie. We both did.

MAD JACK: Wait a minute. How?

JASPER: It's my bit of bush. And you seen me goin' there for years. And I was there that night. Both of us were. And we saw you do it and then scratch sorry into the tree later on. We saw you, dint we, Charlie?

CHARLIE *gives a hesitant nod.*

MAD JACK: Jasper, he couldn't have seen it. It was too long ago.

JASPER: It was three weeks ago.

MAD JACK: What was?

JASPER: Listen old man, we know you killed Laura.

MAD JACK: Laura?

JASPER: The girl you beat and hanged and everything else you did to her. We know it was you, you sick old cunt. And don't act like you don't know her. You seen her walkin' with me all these times, you called out my name every night like a fuckin' lunatic. And now she's dead. And you know why. So just man up and admit it.

MAD JACK: You mean that young girl who's gone missing? Have they found her?

JASPER: *We* found her.

MAD JACK: She's dead?

JASPER: *You know she's dead!*

MAD JACK: Jasper … That is a bloody lie. Strike me. Are you playing games? Is that little girl really dead? You tell me the truth now, boy.

JASPER: You said you did it! Before! You said you'd killed someone!

MAD JACK: Jesus. You've got no idea who I am, do you?

He reaches into his pocket and pulls out a photograph. He hands it to JASPER. MAD JACK *points to the image.*

That there, that's your father. That's your mother. And right there between them, that little baby—that's you.

JASPER *looks at the photograph, confused.*

Jasper, I'm your granddad.

CHARLIE: What?

JASPER: That's bullshit. There's no fuckin' way.

MAD JACK: Your dad David … is my son.

CHARLIE: What? Jasper—

JASPER: You're a fuckin liar. He's fuckin' lying.

MAD JACK: I'm your grandfather, Jasper. I am.

JASPER: You're a sick fuck, that's what you are.

MAD JACK: Your mother—

JASPER: *You shut up about my mum!*

> *He grabs* MAD JACK *violently and shoves him down, raising his fist.*

You don't know fuck-all about her. I'll kill you, you sick old cunt! I'll fuckin' kill you like you killed Laura!

CHARLIE: Jasper!

JASPER: *I'll fuckin' kill you!*

MAD JACK: *Then kill me!* But before you do, hear me out. Please.

> JASPER *stands over* MAD JACK, *still grasping him ferociously, his fist raised ready to strike.* MAD JACK *continues …*

A long time ago your dad David—my son—fell in love with a black woman. Rosie.

> JASPER *loosens his grip on* MAD JACK *a little.*

I didn't approve. And when Rosie got pregnant—with you—well, I told them they could either get rid of you or I'd get rid of them.

> *A beat.* JASPER *glares down at* MAD JACK, *wide-eyed.*

They chose you, Jasper. So I banished all three of you from my life. And when my son finally married your mum, he took her surname— Jones.

> JASPER *slowly lowers his fist.*

The rest of the town turned their backs on them too. And that's around the time your old man started drinking. And your mum, God bless her, decided the only way to reconcile the whole situation was to reach out to me. Every week for a whole year, your mum would invite me round for Sunday dinner. And for a whole year I said no.

> *He stands warily.* JASPER *lets him.*

But I was lonely too, my boy. And I was curious to meet you. So one Sunday I turned up. David pushed past me and went straight down the pub, but your mum … she sat me down and fed me and continued to do so every Sunday after that.

A beat.

She was beautiful. Funny. Brave. She loved you like I've never seen a mother love a child before.

A beat.

Then one Sunday, Rosie and I were halfway through our dinner when she clutched her side. Something was wrong with her insides. She could barely breathe. So I bundled her and you into the Hillman and we took off.

The headlights of the car illuminate.

I went too fast, Jasper, do you remember? I was going so fast. I hit a pothole on the gravel road out of town and we smashed into a tree. You were thrown clear and landed with barely a scratch. Except that one.

He points to the scar on JASPER*'s arm.* JASPER *looks stunned.*

I broke my leg. And your mum … your mum died right there in my car.

A long beat.

Your dad never forgave me. Never let me see you again. I never forgave myself. I keep the wreck of the car in the backyard as a reminder. Scratched the word 'Sorry' into it with a coin when it got delivered to me. It was all I could do. This fucking town … this fucking town who never had a place in their hearts for your mother, suddenly saw me as her killer. So I decided to shut myself away from 'em. Leave 'em to their gossip. The only people I see are the kids who steal my peaches and you … when you wander past.

JASPER *and* MAD JACK *stare at one another.*

I'm sorry, Jasper. I didn't hurt your little friend. But I did kill your mother.

JASPER: You're my grandfather?

MAD JACK *nods.*

MAD JACK: I'm sorry. You can kill me now.

Silence. JASPER *stares at* MAD JACK. CHARLIE *watches on wide-eyed.*

JASPER: Charlie. Go home.

CHARLIE: But, Jasper—

JASPER: I said go home.

CHARLIE: Did you … wanna come with me?

JASPER *shakes his head.*

CHARLIE *looks worried.* JASPER *and* MAD JACK *stare at one another intently.*

Are you okay?

JASPER: I'm fine. Just go.

MAD JACK: Go home, Charlie. We'll be right.

CHARLIE: Yes, Mad Jack.

He gasps.

Sorry! Mr Lionel. Sorry.

JASPER *warily follows* MAD JACK, *leaving* CHARLIE *alone.*

Distant fireworks light the sky.

CHARLIE *speaks to us …*

Nineteen sixty-six. Happy New Year.

The sound of moaning climaxes with the exploding fireworks. CHARLIE *makes his way warily toward the sound in the shadows. He watches wide-eyed for a moment, then …*

Mum!

MRS BUCKTIN *disentangles from a* STRANGER—*his hat is low over his face.*

MRS BUCKTIN: Go, Gus. I'll catch up.

The STRANGER *departs hurriedly.*

CHARLIE: What are you doing? Who's that?

MRS BUCKTIN: What are *you* doing?

CHARLIE: Who's *that*, Mum?

MRS BUCKTIN: You should be at the Miners' Hall!

CHARLIE: Why aren't you?!

MRS BUCKTIN: You are coming home with me. You shouldn't be out here!

She grabs him roughly. CHARLIE *pulls away.*

CHARLIE: And neither should you. This … *this* means I don't have to do what you say anymore.

MRS BUCKTIN: Yes you do, young man. Get home now. I won't ask you again.

CHARLIE: You didn't ask. You never ask me anything.

MRS BUCKTIN: Charlie—

CHARLIE: You dug this hole, Mum. You fill it in. I'm not going home tonight.

MRS BUCKTIN: Charlie!

A long moment.

Your father and I don't love each other anymore. We … lost it somewhere. He's more in love with that bloody book than he is with me.

CHARLIE: What book?

MRS BUCKTIN: You think he's sitting in that nursery mourning our dead child? No. That's my job. He's writing a book.

CHARLIE: What about?

MRS BUCKTIN: Oh … the Great Australian Novel, Charlie.

CHARLIE: The Great Australian Novel? [*To us*] But that's what I'm writing. [*To his mother*] What's it about?

MRS BUCKTIN *speaks numbly.*

MRS BUCKTIN: I reckon it's set in a town of never-ending fucking silence. Silence and space. Dead paddocks and dried-up dams and a bunch of ghosts covered in dust walking around a place where nothing ever changes. It just doesn't fucking change. Stinking men and bored women and incessant heat and filthy flies and fucking on a back seat. Just to feel something, just to feel anything, just to escape the silence. It's about a town that kills women. Murders little girls. A town that even my baby daughter didn't want to be born into. I reckon that's what it's about. Your father's Great Australian Novel. Maybe he's wrapping it all up with a happy ending? That'd be nice, hey? But you know what I reckon, Charlie? I reckon he hasn't written a damn word. Because that's his way. Silence and space.

CHARLIE: He saved Mr Lu the other night, Mum. After those blokes tore up the garden.

> *She smiles sadly.*

MRS BUCKTIN: Did he? What a superhero, hey?

> *Silence.*

CHARLIE: Get your friend to take you home, Mum. We can talk tomorrow.

> CHARLIE *starts to walk away.*

MRS BUCKTIN: Charlie …

> CHARLIE *turns.*

I won't be here tomorrow. I'm leaving Corrigan.
CHARLIE: What?
MRS BUCKTIN: I'm going.

> *A beat.*

Look after your dad for me.

> *A beat.* CHARLIE *nods.*

CHARLIE: I will.
MRS BUCKTIN: And make sure he looks after you.

> CHARLIE *nods.*

One day you'll understand. About all this.
CHARLIE: I hope so.

> *A beat.*

Mum … do you even know how to play bridge?

> MRS BUCKTIN *laughs genuinely.*

MRS BUCKTIN: You're a good man, Charlie. I love you, my darling. Sorry.

SCENE TEN

A new voice on the breeze … that of ELIZA, *singing 'Que Será Será'.*

CHARLIE *follows the sound until he arrives at the curtain of wattle. He opens it. Lights on the glade.* ELIZA *is sitting in a nightgown beside the dam.*

CHARLIE: Laura?
ELIZA: It's me, Charlie. Eliza.

CHARLIE: What are you doing here?

> *She glares at him.*

Have you got the Mean Reds?

> ELIZA *stands up angrily.*

ELIZA: You didn't come back. You promised me you'd come back. The fireworks are over.

CHARLIE: I'm sorry.

ELIZA: How do I know I can trust you if you don't do what you say?

CHARLIE: I'm sorry, Eliza. I had to …

ELIZA: If you'd taken me with you I'd have told you everything.

> *She turns from him.*

CHARLIE: Eliza … how do you know about this place?

> *A beat.*

ELIZA: This …

> *She turns to face* CHARLIE.

This is where Laura died.

> CHARLIE *looks shocked.*

CHARLIE: You know? How?

ELIZA: Because I killed her, that's why.

> CHARLIE *is stunned.*

CHARLIE: Wh … what do you mean?

> ELIZA *struggles to speak.*

ELIZA: This … this is what happened.

> *A beat.*

Every night, from my bedroom, I'd hear Jasper Jones come to Laura's window and tap gently. I'd hear them talk softly to each other. And then she'd climb through the window and follow him away to wherever it is they went.

> *A beat.*

I'd peek out of my window and watch them walk away together, Laura and Jasper Jones. I liked the way my sister's face would change when he came to find her. She'd stopped smiling a long time ago, you see. But when she walked with Jasper Jones, she changed. Her face shone like the moonlight. She was so beautiful, walking barefoot in her nightgown.

A beat.

Don't you think my sister was beautiful?

CHARLIE: She was.

ELIZA: But then Jasper Jones just stopped coming. Laura waited and waited for him. I waited too, in the bedroom next door, listening for his tap on her window. She waited for days and days and days. Laura got really thin. Like she was trying to starve herself of something. She started to disappear before our eyes.

A beat.

Then one night, I heard sounds in Laura's room. My father was in there … I heard an argument. I heard her yell at him in a voice I'd never heard before. I heard a loud thud and the door slam. And then I heard Laura sobbing for a long time. Then her window opened.

ELIZA starts to walk across the stage as LAURA.

CHARLIE: Eliza?

ELIZA: This is what happened. I saw her climb out. Her face was beaten. There was blood on her nightgown.

She walks, as if in a trance. CHARLIE *follows.*

She walked away from our house. By herself in the middle of the night.

She turns to glance at CHARLIE.

I followed.

They walk on, slowly.

I followed her, Charlie. It felt like I followed for an eternity. And Laura didn't look back. Not once.

ELIZA carries on the familiar path as CHARLIE *follows her.*

CHARLIE: Where did she go?

ELIZA: I followed her all the way to here.

CHARLIE: Was there anyone else here?

ELIZA: No. Just me and her.

CHARLIE: What did you say to her?

ELIZA: Nothing. I said nothing. I just crouched in the shadows and watched her.

CHARLIE: What was she doing?

> ELIZA *can't answer.*

Eliza?

ELIZA: She wrote a letter. Then she cried. For a really long time.

> *A beat.*

CHARLIE: Eliza—

ELIZA: This is what happened. My sister stood up. She climbed that tree.

> *She walks to the tree.*

She walked across this branch.

> *She walks beneath the branches.*

She tied a rope around her neck. And she jumped.

CHARLIE: What?

ELIZA: It all happened so fast, Charlie. I ran to her but it was too late. I couldn't get her down. At her feet was the letter she wrote. I read it right there beside her body.

> *She offers* CHARLIE *the letter.*

It's for Jasper. She thought he'd taken off without her and she wasn't going to see him again. So she wrote out everything. About her life. About her family. About the fact that every night for years my father had been sneaking into her bedroom. The room right next to mine, Charlie. About the things Dad did to her in there. About the baby my father had left inside her. About the beating she'd gotten when she spoke up. About why she had to go. And about how much she loved Jasper and that she was sorry she couldn't say goodbye.

> CHARLIE *takes the letter but doesn't read it.*

And then Jasper Jones appeared. Out of nowhere. He just slipped through the wattle like he was returning home. He didn't see me, but he saw Laura hanging there. And he ran to her. And he tried so hard to get her down, to hold her weight, to give her air. But she was gone. So you see, Charlie. I killed her.

CHARLIE: You didn't kill her, Eliza. She killed herself.

ELIZA: I didn't help her, Charlie. I'm no different to Jenny Likens who watched her sister get locked up and beaten and drowned and branded. I didn't help. I just became part of the secret. While my sister was hanging from that tree, I snuck away. When Jasper wasn't looking. I went home. Crawled back through my window and went to bed. Like the gutless killer I am.

> ELIZA *weeps. She sits beside the tree—the word 'Sorry' is illuminated beside her. She touches it.*

CHARLIE: It was you who wrote 'Sorry' on the tree.

> ELIZA *nods.*

ELIZA: I came back a few days later. I had to tell her. I thought she'd still be hanging there. But she wasn't. Then I heard voices. It was you and Jasper Jones.

> *She glares at him.*

Why didn't you tell me you were friends with him, Charlie?

CHARLIE: I'm sorry.

ELIZA: What did he do with my sister? Where did he take her?

CHARLIE: We. It was both of us. We got her down. And we put her in there.

> *He points at the dam.*

ELIZA: You put my dead sister in a fucking dam?

> CHARLIE *nods.*

You knew where she was all this time and didn't tell me?

CHARLIE: Jasper thought someone had murdered her. She was so beaten up. I saw her face with my own eyes, Eliza. We knew Jasper would get the blame. This is his place. So we decided to put her in the dam till we worked out who did it. I wanted so badly to tell you, Eliza. But I made a promise to Jasper too.

ELIZA: Why did Jasper stop coming to my sister's window? Did he not love her anymore? Why did he stop?

> JASPER *appears.*

JASPER: What's she doing here?

> ELIZA *stands, on guard.*

ELIZA: Why did you leave my sister?

JASPER: [*to* CHARLIE] What's she doing here?

ELIZA: How could you just stop turning up like that?

JASPER: I trusted you, Charlie.

ELIZA: She needed you.

JASPER: What's she doing here?

ELIZA: You dumped her in a dam.

CHARLIE: It wasn't just him, Eliza.

JASPER: Get out of my place.

ELIZA: How could you do that to her?

CHARLIE: Eliza, I can explain—

JASPER: I said get out of my place.

CHARLIE: Jasper Jones came to my window.

ELIZA: Trying to save your own skin, you gutless half-caste.

CHARLIE: Eliza!

JASPER: *I said get out of my place!*

> *Silence.* JASPER *looks like he could kill.*

This is *my* place. This here. Not yours. Not yours. Not even Laura's. It's mine. And I'm sick of you people turnin' up and shiftin' everything around and then expectin' me to be able to find my way through it all.

> *A beat.*

This is *my* place.

> *A beat.*

Now get out and leave me alone. I gotta work this out.

> CHARLIE *steps forward nervously.*

CHARLIE: Jasper … Laura wasn't murdered.

> *He hands* JASPER *the letter.*

This is what happened.

> JASPER *takes it. He reads it. Silence.*

> *Then …* JASPER *runs for the dam.*

Jasper!

> CHARLIE *struggles with* JASPER. *It is long and violent. Finally,* JASPER *succumbs, sobbing.*

CHARLIE *holds a protective arm around* JASPER. JASPER *speaks quietly.*

JASPER: I didn't know. I didn't know any of that. All I knew was she wanted to get out. And so did I.

A beat.

I didn't leave her. I just went away to find some work. I brought back enough money to run away to the city with Laura, just like we always wanted. I was gonna take her away from this town. From her room. Everything.

A beat.

Why didn't she just wait?

A beat.

Why didn't she just wait?

ELIZA *stands at a distance looking into the dam.*

ELIZA: She'll wait down there. Forever.

SCENE ELEVEN

CHARLIE: The police decided that Laura had run away.

We visit her at the dam all the time. I work on my Great Australian Novel, Eliza proofreads my words, and Jasper … well, Jasper just sits by the water. He was never really the same after he heard what happened to Laura. Why she did do what she did that night?

Eliza never said anything to the police that summer, but she did show her mother Laura's letter.

She told her mother that if she came forward and told the truth about what had happened in the Wishart house, Eliza would take her to where Laura lay. Until then, Eliza would stay silent. Neither of them have spoken.

MR BUCKTIN *hands* CHARLIE *a book, scruffs his hair, and walks on, looking very different.*

My father finished his book. I'm halfway through it and it's pretty good. He's also gotten rid of his comb-over and is wearing a rather impressive moustache. And the other day he bought a pair of flairs!

We talk about all sorts of stuff, even about Mum and what she's getting up to in the city.

JEFFREY *appears with a plate of watermelon.*

The Lu's watermelon patch grew furiously. Which, I guess, was lucky, because despite his forty-three on debut, Jeffrey was relegated to twelfth man once more. He spent his weekends sharing watermelon with the spectators when he really should've been on the field where he belonged.

A beat.

Fortunately, I had a cunning plan.

SCENE TWELVE

JEFFREY: You're gonna do what?!

CHARLIE: I'm gonna get five peaches from Mad Jack Lionel's tree.

JEFFREY: Charlie, that's crazy. No-one's ever got that many in one hit. You've never even gone near Mad Jack Lionel.

CHARLIE: I've got to. I made a deal with Warwick Trent. If I steal five peaches this very afternoon in broad daylight, I will be granted immunity from his bullying for a full school year. No matter how deep I delve into my vocabulary, no matter how tempting it is for people to tease me about Mum's reputation, I will have immunity.

JEFFREY: Whoa …

CHARLIE: Also, my friend, I have managed to work into the wager a sweet deal for you. If I get these peaches today, you, Jeffrey Lu, will play the remainder of the cricket season as opener. Not twelfth man. And you will also get to bowl in at least one fixture a week.

JEFFREY: Charlie, I appreciate the gesture, but you are batshit insane! You'll die! I haven't even taught you the Bruce Lee one-inch punch yet. Lay back and think of England, Chuck, cos you're about to get royally fucked.

CHARLIE: Oh, ye of little faith. Watch me …

He strides up to Mad Jack Lionel's house.

He turns to us …

The kids of the town are gathering.

JASPER *watches from afar.* WARWICK *sneers from the sidelines.*

They've come to see Charlie Bucktin, Corrigan's coward, fail dismally.

He leans into us.

What they don't know is that Mad Jack Lionel and I have become pretty close over the summer. I go to his house every Sunday for dinner, in fact. And we've hatched a little plan for this afternoon.

CHARLIE *gives a surreptitious wink to the house, then makes his way toward the peach tree. He reaches up and the kids count as he picks each peach.*

ALL: One …
       Two …
       Three …
       Four …
WARWICK: Six …

The other kids shake their heads at him.

ALL: Five.

Suddenly … MAD JACK LIONEL *comes charging out, waving a rifle. He screams …*

MAD JACK: Who's stealing me peaches, then? I'll shoot ya, ya bastard!

CHARLIE *drops the fruit and the crowd screams in terror.*

CHARLIE *puffs up his chest and strides up to* MAD JACK. *He wrestles the rifle from his hand and tosses it aside. Everyone gasps.*

MAD JACK *attacks* CHARLIE *again—he pretends to strangle him as they weave around the yard.* CHARLIE *calls to* JEFFREY *in a strained voice …*

CHARLIE: Jeffrey! The … one-inch … punch!

JEFFREY *looks stunned. He marches forward and faces* MAD JACK.

MAD JACK *shoves* CHARLIE *aside and scowls at* JEFFREY.

MAD JACK: I've shat bigger than you, ya little bastard.

A beat.

JEFFREY *takes up his Bruce Lee stance. He growls.*
Then …

He strikes at MAD JACK.

A beat.

MAD JACK *glances at* CHARLIE *who nods surreptitiously.*

MAD JACK *staggers backward dramatically and falls to the ground, clutching his heart and waving his fist.*

JEFFREY *looks as stunned as the rest of the crowd, but that doesn't stop him asserting himself.*

JEFFREY: I went easy on him. He's pretty old.

CHARLIE *stands tall over* MAD JACK.

CHARLIE: Mad Jack Lionel, I'm takin' your peaches whether you like it or not!

MAD JACK *whimpers and crawls back inside.*

CHARLIE *turns proudly to the crowd, like Superman.*

He gathers the dropped fruit and swaggers back to the crowd.

JASPER *watches from afar, grinning.*

JEFFREY: Holy shit, Charlie! That was amazing! He just came at you with a fucking gun! You should be dead! You're Batman. No, you're better than Batman. You're fucking Superman! Nah, fuck that—you just invented a whole new class of superhero …!

CHARLIE: Couldn't have done it without you, Jeffrey.

JEFFREY: Happy to be of help, Chuck. Five peaches! That's a Corrigan record!

CHARLIE: Well, you gotta get brave at some point, Jeffrey. You gotta get …

He turns to see JASPER *is gone.*

Smoke.

Sirens.

SCENE THIRTEEN

The Wishart house is on fire.

ELIZA *stands in front of it as ash falls around the townsfolk.*

CHARLIE: Eliza!

>*She stands, trance-like.*

ELIZA: It's okay, there's no-one in there.
CHARLIE: What happened?
ELIZA: I just … I just wanted to hurt somebody, Charlie …

>*They watch the house burn.*

CHARLIE: The flames die down after an hour, leaving the Wishart house exorcised and turning Corrigan crimson. It doesn't take long before the town starts to mutter about who was responsible for the fire that burnt the Wishart house to the ground. No-one suspected Eliza. And it doesn't take long for them to start whispering loudly, 'Jasper Jones'.

But what they don't know is that Jasper is already long gone. I can feel it, in my guts. And they'll keep looking for him to blame, but pretty soon, they'll have to look at themselves instead.

I leave them to their gossip and I put my arm around Eliza. Because I've finally got the right words. Not from a book. Or a poem. Words that come from me.

And they're just for her …

>CHARLIE *whispers in* ELIZA*'s ear.*

>*She nods.*

>*They kiss softly and walk away from the embers of the house.*

SCENE FOURTEEN

JASPER *is at Charlie's window.*

He takes a pair of boots from his rucksack and places them beneath the sill, along with a bottle of whiskey and a writer's journal.

JASPER *walks away, leaving Corrigan far, far behind.*

THE END

ALSO BY KATE MULVANY
AND AVAILABLE FROM CURRENCY PRESS

Masquerade, based on the book by Kit Williams
In a wondrous world of riddles and hidden treasure, bumbling Jack Hare is on a race against time to deliver a message of love from the Moon to the Sun. Far, far away in a world just like ours, a mother cheers her son Joe with the tale of Jack Hare's adventure. But when Jack's mission goes topsy-turvy, Joe and his mum must come to the rescue, and the line between the two worlds becomes blurred forever. Bringing to life Kit Williams' iconic picture book, *Masquerade* stars a talking fish, a tone-deaf barbershop quartet, a gassy pig, a precious jewel and a few mere mortals. It's a magical adventure that is, at its heart, about the love between a parent and a child.
ISBN 978-1-92500-540-0

The Seed
Meet Rose Maloney. Her dad Danny went to Vietnam. Her grandfather Brian is ex-IRA. Today is their collective birthday. From this intimate reunion, *The Seed* opens itself up over and over again until a silent family battle becomes a national story about finding new life amongst the rubble of old wars. This play has a very special kind of honesty and humour to it which sorts the great lies we buy into from the reality we live through. A compelling, tightly-woven and thrilling exploration of a very real family and the repercussions of war.
ISBN 978-0-86819-826-2

The Web
Is a person still isolated if their friends are make-believe? Fred is a 16-year-old living on a farm without stock or crops in an Australian country town. When Travis, the charismatic head boy at their school, begins to take an interest in him, Fred gets lured into the intricate world of The Web, where nothing, and nobody, is what they seem. A whodunit for the modern age, *The Web* is a fascinating exploration of isolation, friendship, and what happens when social experiments go frighteningly wrong.
ISBN 978-0-86819-911-5

www.ingramcontent.com/pod-product-compliance
Lightning Source LLC
Chambersburg PA
CBHW041754010726
47507CB00009B/391